Trickle-Down

Timeline

D1520916

Trickle-Down Timeline

short fiction
by

Cris Mazza

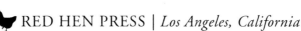

RED HEN PRESS | *Los Angeles, California*

Trickle-Down Timeline
Copyright © 2009 by Cris Mazza

Design assistance by Sydney Nichols

ISBN: 978-1-59709-133-6
Library of Congress Catalog Card Number: 2008942403

The California Arts Council and National Endowment for the Arts partially support Red Hen Press.

www.redhen.org
Published by Red Hen Press
First Edition

Acknowledgements

Acknowledgements made to the following publications in which these pieces first appeared:

The Art of Friction, University of Texas Press for "Trickle-Down Timeline"; *Homewrecker*, Soft Skull Press for "Change the World"; *Inappropriate Random*, Seal Press for "Cookie"; *Scoring from Second*, University of Nebraska Press for portions of "Each Other's History" (published as "My Life in the Big Leagues"); *Strictly Casual*, Serpent's Tail Press (UK) for "Cookie"; *Bridge* for "Trickle-Down Timeline"; *Caprice* for "What Satisfies People"; *Cottonwood* for "Disguised as Suicide"; *Furious Fictions* for "First Year in Meadville"; *Night Train* for "What If"; *North American Review* for portions of "Each Other's History" (published under a different tile); *Pacific Coast* for "The Three Screwdrivers"; *Other Voices* for "What Satisfies People"; *Santa Monica Review* for "Each Other's History"; *Sou'wester* for "Proportion"; *Tarasque II* for "Another Honeymoon Over"; and *Western Humanities Review* for "They'll Shoot You."

Thanks to http://www.quickchange.com/reagan/ for making Reagan-era research more fun.

Contents

Author's Foreword

By now, nostalgia for the 1980s is an established sphere dedicated mostly to reminiscence about music, movies, TV shows, fads and styles of the decade, geared toward those who were in junior high or high school during the '80s. What this kind of nostalgia seems to say is that to these "children of the '80s" (who were, after all, children *in* the '80s), the only things that concerned them were music, movies, TV shows, fads and styles. In this way, most popular observations about the '80s tend to support mainstream media's generalized summary which refers to the '80s as the decade of excess, of consumerism, of superficiality, of the "me-generation." What is missed, forgotten or disregarded by this kind of accepted emblematic synopsis is that there were other people in the '80s who were struggling, and not just financially. For some people, the surplus and glut were part of some other world, not theirs; and it couldn't be a "me-generation" if they didn't know who they were or where they were going. They were often just finding out what they were going to want; or they were, in starting out, already where they were going to end up.

Cris Mazza

Why Not Have an Actor for a Governor?
We Had a Clown the Last 8 Years!

Bumper sticker during Reagan's first campaign
for Governor of California, 1972

Trickle-Down Timeline

1980

Pac-Man became the first computer game hero. He was originally supposed to be Puck-Man (he was, after all, shaped like a hockey puck), but with the threat that rampaging youth might scratch out the loop of the P to form an F on arcade machines, Pac-Man was born, a name with literally no meaning.

Median household income: $17,710.00
Median cost of a house: $76,400.00
These things hardly mattered, or even meant anything to anyone who was just moving out of his or her parents' house and had found an apartment for $200/month which could be afforded on a $100-a-week part- time minimum wage paycheck while finishing a fifth and sixth year of college.

Ted Bundy was sentenced to death by electrocution.

Brooke Shields purred in her Calvin Klein advertisement: *You know what comes between me and my Calvins? Nothing!* Shields also showed off what she had to offer as an actress in *The Blue Lagoon*. Anyone who went on their first date with the person he or she eventually married will remember this film, especially if either of them had to go see it twice because in the middle of the first time, one of their brand new bought-with-birthday-money soft contact lenses came out, and for some reason they still wanted to see how the movie ended.

Ronald Reagan visited the White House to get his job briefing from President Carter. Carter would subsequently disclose that the President-elect asked hardly any questions and did not take notes.

John Lennon was shot, ostensibly for being a phony, by a fan carrying *The Catcher in the Rye*. Doctors at the emergency room that received Lennon's dying body later said they could not have recognized him.

In fact there were few people less phony. As an emblematic death, it was the end of rebellion. Some people, though, were in the throes of being engaged, pawning high school rings to buy silver wedding bands.

1981

The hostages held in Iran for over a year were released on the day of Ronald Reagan's Presidential inauguration. In his inaugural speech, Reagan took credit for the release.

The public heard the first news report about a gay man's mysterious death from an immune-deficiency disease. Later when the media continued reports of the endemic, the disease was defined as one that affected "homosexual men, intravenous drug users and Haitian men." The inclusion of Haitian men in this early description was eventually dropped without explanation.

Striking air traffic controllers were fired by President Reagan.

The Army suggested, *Be All You Can Be*.

The Reagan administration tried to count ketchup as a vegetable in subsidized school lunches.

The minimum wage was raised to $3.35. At forty hours a week, for fifty-two weeks a year, this would net $6,968, no taxes. The poverty threshold for 1981, for a single person, was $4,620. Two-thousand three-hundred forty-eight dollars of breathing room for the year. Some people, however, went to college, and could now make $10,000 a year working behind a desk at a hospital, or as a salesman (person) for a cement company, or as a first year elementary school teacher, or even earn a little more than that as a grocery checker.

Reagan Budget Director David Stockman said in an interview for *Atlantic Monthly*, "None of us really understands what's going on with all these numbers." He then conceded that trickle-down economics "was always a Trojan horse to bring down the top [tax] rate." And then, regarding the tax bill, "Do you realize the greed that came to the forefront? The hogs were really feeding."

Britain's Prince Charles married Princess Diana on live TV, and Americans began a(nother) immersion into Royal-watching. Some other people got married this same year. Some of them did so without the Diana-style wedding dress and hundred-yards-of-lace train. A few of them opted for a minister's office on a Thursday night, the bride wearing a brown corduroy skirt, the groom in white jeans (his best pants).

"Honey, I forgot to duck," Ronald Reagan supposedly said to Nancy after he was shot by John Hinkley Jr. It was immediately assumed that John Hinkley was crazy.

1982

Bob Jones University, which did not allow admission of non-white students, was granted a tax-exempt status by the Reagan administration. A few months later, Reagan told Chicago high school students that the plan was not designed to assist segregated schools because "I didn't know there were any. Maybe I should have, but I didn't."

The poverty rate rose to 15% and the national unemployment rate reached 10.8%. There was a new plan, under consideration by the Reagan administration, to tax unemployment benefits. According to a spokesman, it would "make unemployment less attractive."

President Reagan did not like the media constantly reporting about economic distress. "Is it news that some fellow out in South

Succotash someplace has just been laid off, that he should be interviewed nationwide?" He would have been pleased to hear that after six years of college, some people considered themselves fortunate, almost blessed, to be allowed to teach college composition for $250 per month per class; or rewarded to have started at box boy as an undergraduate and in six short years had become night manager.

An ad from Mattel for children's computers said, *Now you can get a smarter kid than Mom did.* Did college composition teachers discuss the ungrammatical awkwardness of this sentence? And why was Mattel advertising computers for children when some people, even those who taught college composition, were still using electronic typewriters with "correctible" lift-off letters?

Responding to the buzz regarding Nancy Reagan's appetite for fancy gowns, a White House spokesman said that the First Lady's only intention was to help the national fashion industry. Some people, especially those who rode bikes to work—without making a connection or considering it a protest—stopped wearing skirts entirely (even that brown corduroy wedding skirt).

Bottles of Tylenol were laced with cyanide in Chicago area stores and pharmacies. Seven people with headaches died of poisoning.

The Equal Rights Amendment also died.

4150 followers of the Rev. Sun Myung Moon, (2075 of them women), were married in a mass ceremony in Madison Square Garden.

"You know," Ronald Reagan reportedly said to the Lebanese foreign minister, "your nose looks just like Danny Thomas's."

1983

The Navy thought maybe it should eliminate expenses such as $780 screwdrivers, $640 toilet seats, and $9,606 Allen wrenches.

HIV was identified. By this time Haitian men were no longer blamed for carrying the disease. Fashion prognosticators predicted ultra thin would soon not be considered stylish, since those suffering with AIDS were ravaged by weight loss. Plumpness, however, did not find its way into contemporary style. Anyone who was still a virgin in 1980 when they met their future husband, then got married in 1981, was probably not ever going to experience uninhibited sexual experimentation or promiscuity.

Just Say No (also) became the (only) official anti-drug slogan.

The same year Karen Carpenter died of anorexia at the age of thirty-two (which would not do anything to help chubbiness come into fashion), a new pop star named Madonna released her first album. Her voice was compared to Minnie Mouse on helium. Some people, however, weren't buying new albums at the same rate they had when they lived with their parents. So they might own several Carpenters, but no Madonna. One of the Beach Boys also died this year, but no one remembers where they were when they heard Dennis Wilson drowned. This might have meant something, but nobody wondered what.

A White House spokesman said "preposterous" to conjecture about an invasion of Grenada. The following day, because the media was not permitted to cover the mission, the press received, from the White House PR office, photos of Reagan in his pajamas being briefed on the invasion of Grenada.

"I think some people are going to soup kitchens voluntarily," said Ed Meese (who, it turned out, was the same guy who came up with the plan to tax unemployment benefits). "I know we've had considerable information that people go to soup kitchens because the food is free and that that's easier than paying for it . . . I think that they have money."

$3.35 was still the minimum hourly wage.

Ed Meese (whatever his official position, he seemed to do and say a lot), gave a Christmas speech at the National Press Club: "Ebenezer Scrooge suffered from bad press in his time. If you really look at the facts, he didn't exploit Bob Cratchit. Bob Cratchit was paid ten shillings a week, which was a very good wage at the time. . . . Bob, in fact, had good cause to be happy with his situation. His wife didn't have to work. . .He was able to afford the traditional Christmas dinner of roast goose and plum pudding. . . . So let's be fair to Scrooge. He had his faults, but he wasn't unfair to anyone."

1984

Ronald Reagan, preparing for a speech, was asked to test the microphone. He said, "My fellow Americans, I've signed legislation that will outlaw Russia forever. We begin bombing in five minutes."

Penthouse produced its first issue with a man on the cover (George Burns). Inside, the nude centerfold was an underage Traci Lords. In most countries, including the United States, it is (still) illegal to own or view this issue. The same edition includes photos of the first Black Miss America, Vanessa Williams, a few years younger, and nude. Although it was not illegal to look at her photos, Miss America was asked to resign.

Advertisement for Softsoap: *Ever wonder what you might pick up in the shower?*
Advertisement for Sure: *Raise Your Arm if You're Sure.*
Advertisement for Wendy's: *Where's the Beef?*
(Still an) advertisement for the Army: *Be all you can be.*

Despite complaining that it cost too much to administer, Reagan signed the CIA Information Act of 1984, an amendment to the 1966 Freedom of Information Act. At the time the cost of administering the act was less than the Pentagon spent each year on marching bands.

Replacement umpires worked the playoff baseball games when umpires went on strike.

In a Presidential election debate, the former actor pointed out that much of the defense budget was for "food and wardrobe." The Great Communicator went blank in the middle of another answer, then said, "I'm all confused now," before giving his closing statement. Afterwards Nancy beseeched Reagan's aides: "What have you done to Ronnie?" Reagan later claimed that if he'd worn as much make-up as Mondale, he would have looked better in the debate.

The Census Bureau reported that 35.3 million Americans were living in poverty and that it was an eighteen-year high rate of 15.2% of the population. On a televised interview, Reagan said, "You can't help those who simply will not be helped. One problem that we've had, even in the best of times, is people who are sleeping on the grates, the homeless who are homeless, you might say, by choice."

Median household income: $22,415, up 20% since 1980; median cost of a house: $97,600, up 27% since 1980. Minimum wage: still $3.35 / hour; still $6,968 for forty hours of work, fifty-two weeks a year. Some people say this was the best year of their lives. Even some who were right at the median, or even a little below. Especially if things like that didn't matter. Especially since they'd just left home in 1980 and doing their own laundry and grocery shopping—even laundry and grocery shopping for two—was still fun.

1985

In its 100th year, Coca-Cola introduced "New Coke." Three months later, after consumer objection, it reinstated Coca-Cola Classic. Some wondered whether the whole snafu was a planned promotional gimmick.

While most of the American public will only remember The Great Communicator demanding, "Mr. Gorbachev, take down this wall," President Reagan also said, prior his visit to West Germany, that he would not be visiting any site of a former concentration camp because it would inflict too much shame on a country where "very few alive remember even the war." (Whereas American veterans were in their sixties and many of them quite alive) But The White House pronounced that Reagan would lay a wreath at the Bitburg military cemetery, "an integrated home to the tombs of American and Nazi soldiers" (although there are no Americans graves there). President Reagan defended his West Germany itinerary: "I know all the bad things that happened in that war. I was in uniform for four years myself." (His uniform, more aptly called *wardrobe*, was in training films he starred in.)

The number of Barbie dolls sold surpassed the American population. Some people had contributed more Barbie dolls than they would children (as in two dolls to zero children). This helped, because that median income figure was for two people, not three (or four, or five . . .). Even though that wasn't some people's reason for not procreating.

A congresswoman, discussing Ronald Reagan's response to the balanced-budged bill, said, "We tried to tell him what was in the bill but he doesn't understand. Everyone, including Republicans, was just shaking their heads."

A *San Francisco Chronicle* reporter filed suit, under the new Freedom of Information Act, to obtain FBI files that would prove then-California Gov. Ronald Reagan spent years trying to launch an illicit "psychological warfare campaign" against "subversive" students and faculty. The *Chronicle's* questions were referred to Ed Meese (this guy again?), Reagan's chief of staff while he was governor (then too?). Meese said he did not remember planning any such activities. While it would take seventeen years for the *Chronicle* to win the challenge and get documents that in fact proved these things true, in 1985 the FBI only released documents that appeared to have altered Reagan's part as a mole for the FBI in the McCarthy era. Some people, if they'd watched the news more often than ESPN or reruns of *Kung-Fu*, might have wondered if their own activities in the seventies, including visiting a "known commune" (which has the same root word as communism) might have resulted in their own FBI file. But maybe some people knew, without knowing, that it was better to only know now as much as you knew then, when you visited the known-commune not knowing anything except you were there to get some grass.

1986

In thorny contract negotiations with musicians, management of the San Diego Symphony cancelled the season and locked out orchestra members. But even before negotiations officially broke down, management (anticipating the cancellation of the season)—to help pay for the newly refurbished former vaudevillian concert hall—booked shows by East Coast ballet companies, East Coast orchestras, a few comedians, and Barry Manilow.

The first postal killing happened in Oklahoma, netting fourteen postal workers.

Ed Meese (who now, apparently, had a different job) suggested that employers should begin covertly watching their workers in "locker rooms, parking lots, shipping and mail room areas and even the nearby taverns" to apprehend them with drugs. (*Just say no* may not have been working. This was plan B.)

On November 25, as the Iran-Contra scandal simmered, Ed Meese said, "The President knew nothing about it." On November 26, on national television, Meese said, "The President knows what's going on." A month later Meese suggested maybe Reagan did give his approval to the deal, while he was under sedation after surgery.

California Highway Patrol Officer Craig Peyer—who, it turned out, had a history of stopping young women driving alone and talking to them for lengthy periods—pulled college student Cara Knott off the freeway and directed her down a dark, unused off-ramp. Their encounter ended when Peyer strangled Knott and threw her body off a bridge. The day after Knott's disappearance, local TV news chose Officer Peyer to do a safety-on-the-road segment.

An advertisement for Nike said, *Improve your husband's sex life.*
The Army reiterated, *Be All You Can Be.*

The space shuttle Challenger exploded, live on national television. Decades later, a new generation will be defined as those who weren't alive when Kennedy was shot, but who knew exactly where they were when the Challenger blew up. This simplistic division ignores those who not only recall clearly when they heard the Kennedy news (recess cancelled in first grade), *and* when they heard about John Lennon (the afternoon of their last final exam of the fall semester of their senior year of college) but now also remember when the Challenger exploded (while doing sit-ups on the living room floor with the TV on before going back to the laundromat to pick up the white load so there'd be clean underwear for work that evening).

1987

"I hope I'm finally going to hear some of the things I'm still waiting to learn," President Reagan said as the Iran-Contra hearings began. In his January Tower Commission interview about the affair, Reagan conceded that he authorized the arms sale to Iran. In February, Reagan told the Tower Commission that now he remembered that he did not sanction the arms sale. While narrating his (re)recollection from a memorandum, Reagan also read aloud his stage instruction (which some remember to say "be earnest" but they may be confusing it with the time George H. W. Bush read aloud his stage instruction, "message: I care").

President Reagan, in a *Washington Times* interview, reminisced wistfully about the time when Joseph McCarthy and the House Un-American Activities Committee exposed subversives.

The acronym AIDS—first used in 1982 when more than 1,500 Americans were diagnosed with the disease—was not said by Ronald Reagan in public until 1987, by which time 60,000 cases had been diagnosed, and half of those people had died. (Perhaps he was hoping it was still a mysterious disease among Haitian men, and maybe medical research money could go to beefing up immigration laws.) During a rally to protest the administration's (lack of) AIDS policies, Washington police wore large yellow rubber kitchen gloves when they arrested sixty-four demonstrators.

Playtex became the first to use live lingerie models in TV ads for the Cross Your Heart Bra. One might say they tested the waters for panty shield companies who would, in the future, use live actresses to rave about a product that's "not for your period, just those other little leaks."

Gary Hart withdrew from the Presidential race when a sexual misdemeanor was exposed. One might propose that his candidacy died to save the future President Clinton.

At the Iran-Contra hearings, no one, including the President, ever definitively found out what he knew or when he knew it.

Prozac was approved by the FDA. Some people needed it right away. Even anyone who had used audacity, cunning and acumen to successfully fake a psychological exam and earn a 4F draft deferment in 1969—that same someone might come home from an hour on the grocery workers picket line and cry, and be curled up in a fetal ball by the time anyone else came home, and not be able to afford Prozac without health insurance.

1988

The Bureau of Labor Statistics said that more than 6 million persons who worked, or looked for work at least half of the year, had family incomes below the official poverty level in 1987.

President Reagan on Michael Dukakis's campaign for the presidency: "You know, if I listened to him long enough, I would be convinced that we're in an economic downturn, and that people are homeless, and people are going without food and medical attention, and that we've got to do something about the unemployed."

A (new) Nike advertisement said, *Just Do It.*
Visa said, *It's Everywhere You Want to Be.*
The Army continued to say, *Be All You Can Be.*

A General Motors advertisement said, *This is not your father's Oldsmobile.* This campaign was credited with helping hasten the eventual demise of Oldsmobile, as the message confirmed for baby-boomers the notion that Oldsmobile had been a make preferred by their fathers.

One and a half million acres of Yellowstone National Forest burned. For the fortunate who actually had that archetypical '50s and early '60s baby-boomer upbringing, where the family station wagon, festooned with tourist decals, was certain to pull into Yellowstone at least once, this might have signaled the final death of childhood. Just to be certain biological clocks had been completely distorted, Old Faithful began to change its schedule.

Other factors contributing to early midlife-crises might have included the incursion of the first college-educated Gen-Xers into the job market the previous year. College composition teachers had already noticed the atti-tude-change in their students, and the number of business majors who wore Bush campaign pins. Then the morning of the election, when the pedestrian overpass spanning the freeway beside the university was adorned with Dukakis posters, some people actually thought "maybe all is not lost."

In his last television interview as President, when asked to comment on his Presidency overlapping with a sizable upsurge in the number of homeless people, Ronald Reagan wondered if many of these were homeless by "their own choice." He extended this analysis to people without jobs. For the second time he clarified his point by referencing the number of newspaper classified job listings.

1989

A new East German government prepared a law to lift travel restrictions for East German citizens. On November 9, a government spokesman was asked at a press conference when the updated East German travel law would come into force. His answer seemed flustered: "Well, as far as I can see . . . straightaway, immediately." Within hours, tens of thousands of people had gathered at the wall, on both sides. When the crowd demanded the entry be opened, the guards stood back, and the wall was disengaged, peacefully. It's possible the East German plan to allow "private trips abroad," never intended the complete and total opening and then destruction of the wall. Did Ronald Regan, almost one year out of office, try to take credit? (Yes.)

Pro-democracy demonstrators in Tiananmen Square were fired on by Chinese soldiers. Between 400 and 800 people were killed. (Reagan did not take the blame.)

Although he denied betting on baseball games, Pete Rose was banned for life from Major League Baseball. Why does it seem that Tiananmen Square and the Berlin Wall faded from the news quicker than Rose's fall from fame?

Ted Bundy was executed in Florida's electric chair. This event did not muster much outcry. There is still more debate over whether Rose should be allowed back into baseball than the efficacy of the death penalty, although, admittedly, Rose is a slightly better example for debating baseball's betting rules than Ted Bundy is for a discussion of capital punishment. However, while Bundy simply solidified for the Right their belief in society's moral right to kill undesirables, it only caused shades of grey for the Left, some of whom were distracted further by the realization that even mating with someone of the same political persuasion didn't guarantee a sublime unison, and some kinds of disillusionment could not be fixed, even with Prozac.

Since 1980, the median income went up $11,196 or 63%. The median cost of house went up $72,400 or 94%. The overall cost of living rose 48% while minimum wage was still $3.35/hour. If you went to college, but didn't major in business or engineering, medicine or law, you could probably hover right near the median two-person household income of $28,906, provided you sustained two people in the household.

Some people got married this year; actually two million four-hundred-three thousand two-hundred-sixty-eight. A nearly as impressive number, one million one-hundred-fifty-seven thousand, were divorced.

Although, later, the '80s would be called—usually by patronizing college students who'd grown up in soft middle-class homes—the era of superficiality and decadence, some people never got to become yuppies or conspicuous consumers or marital swingers or weekend cokeheads. Maybe they already were all they were going to be.

Proportion

If I was ever going to see him again, of course it would be in San Francisco. We'd been in San Francisco together once another time, at the onset of the '80s, on a chartered bus with an amateur chorus, and he'd said, "When you leave home like this, all you have to do is go 100 miles up the freeway and your life doesn't seem real anymore, everything's out of phase, out of proportion, like worrying late at night."

He was the choir director. I was a mezzo soprano. His marriage was falling apart. I was a virgin. It didn't seem to faze him.

And my life didn't seem real anymore, and I left the singing group soon after that. And heard he and his wife had gotten turned around, had a child, bought a house.

In San Francisco ten years later, at a coffee bar near Davies Hall, I watched him carry his espresso and a newspaper to a table in the corner, fold the paper over, sip from the tiny espresso cup, smooth a crease in the paper with one finger, touch his upper lip with the tip of his tongue.

I stood there long enough, eventually he looked up, must've seen me, didn't smile, stood, waited, holding the silly little espresso mug in his big hand.

The last time we'd been in San Francisco, in the morning, in the hotel cafe, he'd said, "That donut looks so huge. Know what a donut looks like to the rest of us? Trim an inch off your donut, all around the outside. That's what a donut looks like to me."

I got regular coffee, large, cream and sugar, felt him watch me make my way around tables and chairs, but I didn't look up until I had already set my big cup on his table.

I said, "Now my life feels real everywhere I go. Or else it isn't real anywhere. I no longer worry late at night." But I don't know if I said it aloud.

Maybe I said, "Exchange cups with me, then nothing will seem out of proportion to you."

If he did touch my face, his fingers were hot from the espresso.

1980

The New York Times equated heavy traffic with nuclear disaster, explaining the new word for dysfunctional transportation flow: "'Gridlock' is to highway engineers what nuclear meltdown is to nuclear engineers—a panic inside a nightmare inside a worst case."

What Satisfies People

He's been married almost three years. Now Lee's wife thinks he's not satisfied anymore. Something about his bar-be-cue reunion plan has really set her off.

"Did you only marry me to try to forget about *her*?" Joyce asked. "And it took three years to realize it didn't work? Is that why you've been in such a funk?"

He laughed. Joyce never knew his friend Mona, but he's told her everything. Maybe too much.

Just before she left yesterday, Joyce shouted, "What was it about that frumpy flirt that you wanted so badly?"

"I don't know what you mean."

"Can't you even see what she really was?" Joyce screamed. "A religious fanatic, a cock-tease, and a frigid fish, all balled into one. Is *that* what you want?"

He poured some tea and broke the tea pot. "Honey," he said, "you're inventing a problem."

"Bullshit. You're been like a caged animal—you hardly sleep, not to mention everything you've broken or ruined."

She was standing there with a suitcase in front of the television's cracked-open screen. It was a small suitcase. He didn't get up. He was reading a textbook from a business law class he'd taken in college, a tough course that had forced him to work harder than he ever had before. Mona and he had studied together. That was the semester she was taking music history.

One thing he's learned, Joyce isn't very original when she's agitated. "Call me when you figure out what you want."

Mona wasn't very original either. She had said, "Let's keep in touch." Maybe he's the one who said that. He hasn't seen her in eight years. She also said, "It's got to be all or nothing," then she never chose one. One night during their last semester, he was having trouble sleeping and phoned her, his best friend, and when she answered he started talking, telling her things, and when he paused she said, "Who is this?"

There's no use trying to force himself to go to sleep tonight. Falling asleep has always been difficult. Sometimes more so than others. Way back when he was a kid, he started his get-to-sleep method of making up a story, putting himself in it and riding it out, then trying to make *it* be his dream that night. And if you have a doctorate in psychotherapy you call it *fantasy*. But *neurotic* fantasy? He doesn't know. You know what they say: neurotics build castles in the air, psychotics live in them. He used spy stories and sports stories, all adventure and fame. Then in high school the stories were romances, teachers falling in love with him, girls kidnapping him and keeping him as a sex slave with other girls coming to his rescue, bathing his tender wounds. They were real girls he put in the stories, girls that actually existed, but not the girls he knew well enough to talk to. Then for a while, in college, he started using Mona in his bedtime story. She left the story at some point, maybe a few months after graduation. Mona wouldn't keep him as a sex slave, and if she rescued him *from* sex, it would be like admitting she'd never . . . So the story went on without her. It's like a serial that runs anywhere from ten minutes to a half hour when he goes to bed, then he tries to get the story to continue in a dream after he finally falls asleep. But so far he's never dreamed the right things, the things he plans.

It's been a bad month. Ever since Manny Sanguillen retired, Lee started spending a lot of time in the back yard pitching baseballs at a target. He has a bucket of balls. When the bucket is empty, he picks up all the balls at the other end of the yard and brings them back to start over. Sanguillen was the catcher he most would've wanted to pitch to. Soft hands but a wiry competitor. A couple of weeks ago Lee was pretty wild and had to search for most of the balls after he emptied the bucket. While he was out there rooting around, collecting them, he picked up a ball, turned and pitched it through the bedroom window. It was early morning and Joyce was still in bed.

All the stuff he bought for the cook-out is still in a grocery bag in the freezer. Mona's been married longer than he has, and he thought the four of them could play cards or make popcorn and watch a movie. You don't know unless you try. So he broke a few things. They were all accidents.

Maybe he's clumsy or accident-prone. The last time he saw Mona before graduation, he was filling her bicycle tires and blew out *both* of them. Then last night he tapped the teapot spout against the coffee table and it snapped off. The bedroom window and the television screen are broken now, and the front of the refrigerator is dented, but he doesn't think he's careless. Look at the phone: he took it apart and put it back together, but it still works. Joyce begged him to make love to her, so he did a few times, no problem, but she cried. He never thinks about Mona while making love. God knows that would be impossible.

About a month ago his bedtime serial story had one of its frequent big climaxes. This one was a reunion, a college homecoming party or something, where everybody is impressed if you still have your hair or you've published a book, and there're a few old lovers or even friends who catch each other's eyes across the crowd and make their way toward each other. Maybe both of them regret the choices they made that caused them to separate or drift apart; maybe only one of them does, but it's not the one you'd expect. He was wide awake. He never did get to sleep that night, and the serial story stopped right there. He thought about everything.

She had been wearing her black graduation robe, which made her skin even paler, when she said, "Let's keep in touch, Lee." Yes, he's pretty sure she's the one who said it. He wouldn't have been as happy if he'd had to say it. He hadn't listened to any of the graduation speeches, wondering if she would say it. They sat together during the ceremony. For about a month before graduation he hadn't seen her—not since he blew out her bike tires. He didn't know if that was why he hadn't seen her for a month. They didn't say anything, but sat there, and then he asked someone to take their picture together. He had two copies made and was going to give her one. But why was he afraid to call her? He still has the two snapshots.

So eight years later he lay awake all night planning to call her, planning what she would say and what she would do. Just two old friends catching up on lost years. A reunion with a college buddy. What's wrong with that? He thought her first word would be, "*Well!*" He was fairly sure he knew how she would smile. She wasn't very pretty, in the way girls are pretty, but she had a smile. They worked together in the library and studied together after work. They went to McDonald's, listened to records, and sometimes didn't talk but sat reading together, different books, different chairs. She sang in church on Sundays and he went to hear her a couple of times. She always wore plain loose cotton or wool dresses, nothing sleeveless, nothing low-backed or low-necked, everything had a collar and came down to her knees and she wore low-heeled pumps. Her hair was straight and she wore no make-up. They started to discuss religion the same night he first touched her, in his car sitting outside her apartment. He doesn't remember what she said. They never talked about it again. What the hell did they talk about when they talked? She came to his baseball games, then waited while he showered and dressed, and they went to the library together and studied, then went for a hamburger or a pizza. Sometimes they talked, sometimes they didn't. She made him dinner at her place once, and he would fill her bicycle tires every two months or so. Six months after graduation, she married a man who went to her church. They probably have children by now. She can't get divorced—her church doesn't allow it. The guy's stuck with her.

Joyce laughed when he said he was going to invite Mona and her husband over. She said, "How about some *Sunday*? Think they'll fraternize with heathens?" She went to the store with him, the first time, when he bought the barbecue, the redwood table and the lawn furniture. They had it delivered, except the barbecue. It had a twenty-five-page instruction book which he had to study before he could use it. He used a yellow highlighter for the important passages.

Joyce is a schoolteacher. She used to stay after school and mark papers or clean up her classroom. The last few weeks she started coming home earlier, bringing a shoulder bag of arithmetic papers and reading worksheets to mark at home. She would come in the door, throw the bag on the couch and shout, "Lee, what're you doing?" and come hunting for him.

He went alone to the store and bought a tablecloth with green and gold checks. Red and white was too traditional, but flowers seemed inappropriate—it wasn't a wedding reception. He took it out of the package and ironed it, then kept it across the back of the couch so it wouldn't get any new creases.

"You're going to a lot of trouble," Joyce said.

"You have to go to some trouble to get things to turn out right," he said.

"You and Mona are experts on that."

"Just wait," he said. "She's going to look around and say, *all that study-ing paid off, didn't it?* Or, *You've done better than I thought you would.* Or, *Lee—you've changed.*"

"What do you think would've happened if you'd married her?"

He said, "Hand me that thinner, please." He was painting the new redwood table. "We were *friends*."

"Is that what a friend is?" Joyce said. "Someone who suggests you go driving down by the harbor and—"

"All right."

"—says she's cold so you'll put your arm around her, then suggests that you park somewhere, and closes her eyes when you finally kiss—"

"That's enough, Joyce."

"—and the next day says—"

"*Shut up!*" One of the new lawn chairs got stained when he threw the paintbrush.

"Great, now we can't take this stuff back when she doesn't show up."

He chased her into the bedroom. The next morning was when he broke the bedroom window with a baseball. She should've already been up and in the kitchen.

She was crying but not sobbing. "Why couldn't she make up her mind," Joyce said. "Why didn't she just let you fuck her? Why'd she have to half-way seduce you then turn so *holy* all of a sudden? Maybe we'd have some peace now. Maybe we'd have children."

"Calm down, Joyce, it was an accident."

"Why didn't you throw baseballs at *her?*"

"Please, Joyce, it just slipped out of my hand. See—the old curveball still works." He laughed. "Maybe I could've been a pro after all."

"Why are you taking this out on me, Lee? I'm not the one who continually—"

He left her ranting and took a shower. When he came out, she was gone, and her big bag of school papers was gone too. He called his secretary and said he wouldn't be in. He swept up the glass, then planned the menu, then he was rearranging the furniture and pushed the coffee table into the television screen. He decided to move the TV out to the garage when Mona came over. He pictured her coming in the front door, smiling. He would have Joyce beside him, tell them to come in, act friendly and natural, put his arm around Joyce as they all went into the living room. Maybe Mona wouldn't say anything after all, just look at him, sort of an apology.

He called her church and got her phone number by pretending to be someone from the choir who'd just gotten back from five years in Africa. He wrote the number on the pad beside the phone. Joyce slept on the couch. She said the bedroom was too cold because of the broken window. In the morning he went out in his bathrobe and sat on the floor beside the couch. He put his head on her belly and she stroked his hair. "Poor Lee," she said. "You think I don't understand, but I do." She smelled good. He said, "Hmmmm."

"It must've been awful to be so confused," she said.

He put his arms around her and held her tight like he holds his pillow when he's trying to go to sleep. She rubbed his back. That always makes him groan. She said, "I just can't understand why you'd ever want to see her again."

He was going to make the call that day, that afternoon at 5:30, after he got back from buying the steaks and corn-on-the-cob, and ingredients for ice cream. "Everything will finally be okay," he said. "You'll see—we'll be friends again."

She stopped rubbing and sat up. His head slid off her lap. "Again," she said. "You mean the way you were friends when she let you hold her tit and then didn't know who you were two hours later when you called—"

"*Enough!*" There was no baseball around. He pitched a sofa pillow but it didn't even hit anything.

He dialed and Mona answered and he told her his name before he found out if she would know who he was just from his voice saying *Hi.*

"This is Lee!"

"Oh."

He dropped the phone then picked it up. It was still working. He didn't ask if she has kids or where her husband works or if she's still singing. All he asked about was her job and she answered each question with less than three words. He doesn't remember what she said. She didn't ask him anything about anything. He was holding a baseball tight enough to wring water from it, and he threw it, he's not sure when, maybe after his last question, after her last one-word answer. A breeze came through the broken living-room window. He thought he could smell charcoal and lighter fluid. The baseball rolled across the street, into the gutter. He's not sure if he ever actually said goodbye or if he hung up before or after he hit the front of the refrigerator with the phone. But the phone is sitting there now, the receiver in the cradle, so it could ring if someone wanted to call.

Before she left, Joyce also said, "The one good thing you did was blow out her bike tires. Why couldn't it have ended then?"

But it didn't. It didn't end anywhere. It never had an ending. So maybe that's where his serial story will have to pick up from when he goes back to it tonight: *Like gunshots, one after another, the force knocked him backwards, and Mona screamed . . .*

1981

At a Congressional hearing, James Watt responded "Yes," when asked if natural resources should be preserved for future generations. He then added "I do not know how many future generations we can count on before the Lord returns."

Disguised as Suicide

Just before Jan won the title of Miss Sand Valley, California, her agent—who'd driven 200 miles to Sand Valley the day before the contest and signed her on after the preliminaries—whispered in her ear, Tell them you want to be a doctor, that always knocks their eyes out.

The other finalists hugged her and buzzed her cheek with pursed red smiles. The mayor shook her hand and had his picture taken while being pecked on the forehead. Everyone's faces tipped up toward her, applause sounded like bacon frying, cameras clicky-clacked as she traveled down the raised runway and back again. She was thinking about what her new agent had said.

So, she decided, this was not what she was all about. She thanked her new agent and he became her former agent. Instead of going on to bigger contests, she left her agent scowling and went to a trade school for health-field employees because what she'd said was, after all, no lie: Helping other people was more glamorous, deep inside where glamour counts, than becoming a world-class model.

She breezed through her trade-school courses, majoring in hospital administration, because hospitals are not only the most important—she said to whoever it was that took her out to celebrate the night of her graduation—but also the places of biggest need. She pointed out: a dental assistant stands there and hands things to a dentist that he could pick up by himself. A doctor's assistant makes appointments that are never kept on time. A transcriptionist sits typing whatever a doctor says into a tape machine, almost never sees the doctor—nor the patient—and then whatever she types might get filed away somewhere and never looked at again. But hospital administration is a field where you know you're making a difference every day, working side-by-side with a family of caring professionals helping those who need you most.

She got a job. Seven new outfits added to her wardrobe made it possible to not repeat for over three weeks—although, as she'd learned in trade school, that ploy was most effective and important in a geriatric facility with long-term patients where variety and color helped brighten their day, whereas the job she got was at a small neighborhood hospital.

At first she was a trifle disappointed because she had the night shift, eleven pm to seven am—never called *graveyard* in a hospital. The whole facility wouldn't be very active: no surgery planned, no meals served, no one needing counseling or company. She didn't even have to dress up, but at least she was the only administrative employee on duty. The things she would be doing no one else did. She had a little office across the hall from the ER and its small waiting room. The main office and plushly furnished lobby were closed and abandoned at night. Jan typed charts for people who came to the emergency room, typed the new hospital census at midnight, copied and delivered the census to message boxes for doctors and heads of departments, typed the next day's menu and posted it, prepared and mailed insurance bills for outpatients M through P, and answered the main hospital phone if it rang. After a week the thought of either joining the Peace Corps or calling her old agent crossed her mind.

It was a full moon on Monday of the second week.

"We can expect some of our friends tonight," said Ms. Cory, the emergency room nurse.

"A party?" Jan asked.

"No, honey," Nurse Cory laughed. "Repeaters. The suicide attempts."

"Oh! But if we know beforehand, shouldn't we stop them?"

"And ruin their fun?"

Jan found an envelope propped on her typewriter. It was an invitation to a costume party, but she didn't know who was giving the party. The hospital was quiet. Only a little past midnight. She sat looking at the card.

Then it started. The bell sounded on the automatic doors at the end of the hall, the door swung open, and someone was calling "Help us, please!" Jan leaped up, grabbing a blank chart and a clipboard. Nurse Cory was already leading a stumbling man into the emergency room. A woman stood sobbing at the ER doorway.

"Let me help you," Jan said. She guided the woman into the waiting room. When the woman could speak, she just said "here," and handed Jan an insurance card. Jan said, "I'll be right back to talk to you in a while. You'll feel better then."

Jan took the chart, still blank, into the emergency room. Nurse Cory had pulled a curtain around one of the beds. "So you haven't eaten anything for a week and then ran ten miles?"

The man's teeth were chattering, but he said, "She didn't believe me. I told her I was run down, I told her I'd die of exhaustion soon. Next time she'll believe me."

"There are easier ways, you know," Nurse Cory said. Jan could only see the nurse's ankles and feet beneath the curtain. Then she saw the man's pants drop to the floor at the end of the bed.

"She didn't believe me. Now she will."

Nurse Cory came out to answer the phone. The exhausted man called, "Hey!" Jan found a towel, ran cool water over it, then squeezed it out and brought it behind the curtain to the exhausted man. "What's this for," he said, "where'd *she* go?"

"I took care of your wife. She's resting comfortably."

"Not her—the nurse."

Jan folded his pants and put them on a chair beside his bed. She took the pillow from the empty bed beside him, tried to tuck it beneath the pillow already under his feet. The exhausted man was holding the curtain aside, watching Nurse Cory talk on the telephone.

"Was the safety pin opened or closed when you swallowed it, sir?" Norse Cory asked. She doodled on the cover of a magazine. Jan brought her a pad of paper. "Well, did the *pen* have ink in it when you swallowed it?"

When the doors rang and opened again, a cheerful ambulance driver called, "I've got a bleeder here for you." The woman he had on the gurney had deep scratches on her face, neck and arms—scratches in pairs or triplets, running parallel.

"Hello," the woman said. "Where's Doctor Dempsey?"

Jan dialed the number of the attending doctor's room but no one answered. She let it ring twenty times.

Nurse Cory helped the ambulance driver lift the woman onto a bed. "Doctor D. just got a little angry," the woman said.

"Haven't you taken care of that cat's claws yet, Willa?"

"Where's Doctor Dempsey?"

"He's not on tonight," Nurse Cory said. "Doctor Peterson will take care of you."

A doctor came in, yawning.

"He's here!" Jan said, putting the phone down.

"*No, no, no*, I want Doctor Dempsey—he said to call him any time I needed him. He's my only doctor!"

"Here's the perp.," the ambulance driver said, coming back in with a small cage containing a fluffy cat. "She had him all ready to go when I got there."

"Doctor Dempsey," the woman said, smiling, holding her arms out for the cat.

Jan lined the wheelchairs up neatly against one wall so no one would trip over them.

"Call Doctor Dempsey at home," Dr. Peterson said. "Those cuts have stopped bleeding."

The scratches were each at least three inches long and most over a half inch deep. The sides of the cuts lay open like the covers of books. There were also some scabbed-over scratches.

"Doctor Dempsey just went a little crazy, I guess," the woman said, giggling. "Probably just boredom. I named him after my favorite doctor, Doctor Dempsey. He sews me up."

Jan found her clipboard on the scratched woman's bed. The exhausted man's blank chart was still on the clipboard.

"I guess he had nothing better to do," the woman said, and continued smiling. "Dear Doctor Dempsey."

"You know how you get a cat to do that?" the ambulance driver asked the nurse. She was dialing the phone.

"Yep—hold it by the tail and dangle it over your face."

Dr. Peterson went in to see the exhausted man. "Where's the chart on this patient?" The wet towel splatted onto the floor.

"Doctor Dempsey's on his way, Willa," Nurse Cory said. "Wasn't there anything good on television tonight?"

"He said to call him whenever I needed him. Poor old Doctor Dempsey. He'll finally meet his namesake."

The ambulance driver took his gurney and left. "I'll probably be back."

"We'll count on it," Nurse Cory said. She was dabbing antiseptic on the scratches.

Jan rinsed out the exhausted man's damp towel then draped it over the back of a chair to dry. "I've got this ready for when he needs it again."

Dr. Peterson left the room.

"Leave them for Doctor Dempsey to sew up," the woman told Nurse Cory.

"When is someone going to take care of me!" the exhausted man called. Jan went through the curtain to his bedside. "Where's the doctor or nurse?" he said, clutching the sheet up to his chin.

"Is there anything I can get you?"

"The doctor or nurse."

The scratched woman was sitting on the edge of the bed swinging her legs. Nurse Cory was still cleaning scratches.

"I've been talking to the man there," Jan said. "I've got him resting."

Nurse Cory took the cat into the waiting room.

The door rang. A gurney rattled down the hall. "A bleeder here," said another paramedic. "Busy tonight?"

The man on the gurney was slashed—arms, legs, torso, everywhere—with a razor blade.

"I've got the same insurance as last time," the slashed man said.

"Have you been here before?" Jan asked.

"Last month—you kicked me out, remember?"

"I wasn't here last month."

"Get me someone who knows something. Couldn't find anything wrong with me. Does everything have to be as plain as the nose on my face?"

Three young people were clustered at the door of the ER holding onto each other's arms. Nurse Cory was on the phone again. "Try a sleeping pill, it won't kill you."

"May I help you?" Jan asked.

"That's our father."

"Come to the waiting room and you'll be more comfortable. We're taking care of him. He'll be fine, good as new."

The three people sat side-by-side on the couch. The exhausted man's wife was holding a magazine. The cat purred.

"I finally got him to rest," Jan told the wife.

"Are you the doctor?"

Jan typed a chart for the slashed man, brought it to the emergency room and laid it on a table which had been wheeled up next to his bed. Nurse Cory removed the chart to put down a tray of equipment for the doctor. "Damn," Dr. Peterson said. "It's going to take me all night to sew this up."

The exhausted man was calling, "Nurse, why isn't anyone helping me." Nurse Cory was going through the emergency room with an armload of dirty towels, snatched up the damp one hanging over the back of a chair as she passed.

"Let me take them," Jan offered. The nurse dumped the bundle into Jan's arms and went back to grab the ringing telephone. "How long has his jaw been stuck open?" Nurse Cory said into the phone.

Jan didn't know what to do with the towels. The wet one was making her new blouse damp. She found a housekeeper's bucket in the hall and put the towels in it.

"I'm getting mad as hell," the exhausted man was saying.

"Would it help if you had someone to talk to?" Jan asked him.

"It would help if I had a doctor or nurse."

Jan used a paper towel to wipe up drops of water on the floor. "There, now no one'll slip." She'd learned how to squat while wearing a skirt, with her back erect, knees and ankles together. She stood back up upright without needing help from a chair or doorknob.

Nurse Cory had to wash all the slashed man's cuts before the doctor could sew them. "I could show you the right way to do this," she said, "on your wrists, vertically, so it would be more successful."

The slashed man said, "My kids'll be here soon."

"They've already arrived," Jan called from the back counter where she was washing out the sink. "I calmed them down, they're fine." Dr. Peterson came over to wash his hands. Jan had gone out to breakfast with him last week. "This is better than a beauty contest," she said. He dried his hands and went back to the slashed man.

"What do you have for me?" A large man came into the ER wearing a golf sweater over a scrub suit.

"Doctor Dempsey!" the scratched woman screamed. She clapped her hands. "You came for me. I knew you would."

"Ah, Willa, again? If you want to visit me, why not just drop by and say Hi during office hours instead of showing up disguised as an accident?"

"You're always so busy, Doctor Dempsey."

Dr. Dempsey took the scratched woman's chart which Jan was handing to him. He laid it aside without looking at it.

"Where's the doctor, dammit," the exhausted man called.

"Calm down, you're all right." Dr. Peterson didn't even look up from his sewing of the slashed man. "Lie still, will you?"

"I'm trying to see what you're doing."

"Next time just take some pills, okay?"

The scratched woman chortled, "Doctor Dempsey, just wait'll you see my kitten."

Both doctors were sewing. Nurse Cory set up two lamps and directed the bright beams toward the wounds. Then she brought the exhausted man some liquid protein.

"Finally," he said. Then, "Hey, where're you going now!" Nurse Cory went out of the emergency room to get some clean towels.

Jan stacked the three charts neatly on the counter.

The phone rang. Nurse Cory was back. "How many marbles did you swallow, Mr. Carter?"

Jan went to the foot of the slashed man's bed. Dr. Peterson was sewing a long cut that ran from elbow to armpit. "Need a towel for your forehead?" Jan asked. Dr. Peterson didn't answer. The slashed man glared. Jan found a small washcloth, went to the doctor's side and patted his forehead.

"Hey, I can't see what I'm doing!"

"Now you can. I took care of the perspiration for you," Jan said.

"I thought I came here for medical attention," the exhausted man yelled. "I could've died in bed at home and saved myself the trouble of driving down here."

"What's with him," the doctor asked.

Jan said, "I've been in to talk with him several times," and Nurse Cory said, "I gave him the liquid protein a half hour ago."

"Give him more. Maybe you should put it into a baby bottle."

"I heard that," the exhausted man cried. "I'll sue this place, then you'll see."

Nurse Cory went behind the exhausted man's curtain with a small glass and a straw. "My wife should be out there somewhere—worried sick" the exhausted man said.

Jan went into the waiting room. One of the slashed man's children was watching the television. The others were looking at magazines. The exhausted man's wife was smiling gently, flipping through photos in her wallet. The cat was on her lap. Jan went to the exhausted man's wife and touched her arm. "Your husband is going to be fine. We're giving him special fluids. He's resting quietly. I made sure he had two pillows and a cool towel."

"But what's the *doctor* doing?" the wife asked, stroking the cat.

"How about our father," one of the slashed man's children asked.

"I told him you're here. That made him feel more at ease."

"But what's the *doctor* doing?"

"I just told you," Jan said, her voice involuntary flat, then she quickly remembered to let her smile beam again. "That's a cute pin, do you like mine?" She bent to show the exhausted man's wife's the brooch on her blouse—a bunny holding a bunch of flowers. She'd bought it in the hospital gift shop.

Back in the ER, the scratched lady sipped soda from a paper cup and Dr. Dempsey put his equipment away. "I haven't had any mail for a week," she said. "Not even advertisements. Do you suppose something's wrong with the post office?"

"I think something's wrong with your cat," he laughed.

"He didn't mean anything by it. In fact, he didn't seem so angry at all. It's almost as though *I* was the one who was furious instead of Doctor D."

"I think I understand exactly how you must feel," Jan said.

The lady caught Nurse Cory's arm as she was going by. "You know, all night I hear cats fighting around my house."

Jan ran into the hall when the door rang, but it was only an orderly going out for some air. She heard giggling coming from the waiting room. The cat was on the floor doing tricks for cheese crackers from the vending machine. One of the slashed man's children was sorting the exhausted man's wife's photos on the magazine table. The exhausted man's wife was laughing at the cat, wiping tears from her cheeks.

Nurse Cory put down the phone. "Don't leave yet. Dr. Dempsey, we've got another ambulance on its way."

"Doctor Dempsey," the scratched lady called. "These places itch—what should I do! Help!"

Jan found a pen under the counter. "Whoever lost a pen—I found it." She stood holding the pen over her head, careful not to stretch too far and cause her blouse to be tucked into her skirt too loosely and unevenly.

The door rang and blasted open. "There it is," Nurse Cory said. The man on the gurney was propping up his torso with his elbows. One of his pant legs was blood-soaked. "Don't ask me how it happened," he said.

"Has anyone happened to notice what color blouse I'm wearing?" Jan said, "It's sage, the color that reduces violence in prisons."

"He was run over," the paramedic said. "By his own car."

"Stop talking and help me," the man said.

"Said he must've fallen asleep while working on his car," the driver said. "But I don't know . . . no light, no tools, just this guy lying under his own car in the driveway."

"I've been here a full week," Jan said. "How'm I doing so far? Notice, you don't have to tell me what to do anymore."

"Help me, help me—someone get me a doctor! Hey, everyone, come back here!" Jan was the only one left beside the gurney. The nurse had gone to get a thermometer and the paramedic was getting a cup of coffee. Dr. Dempsey was washing his hands, still talking to the scratched lady. "A man's bleeding over here," the man on the gurney called. "Want me to lose this leg?"

"Shut up, shut up," the slashed man yelled.

"Lie still, would you, or I'll sew your mouth closed."

The exhausted man pulled his curtain aside. "I just wanted to see why no one thinks I need any medical care."

"I'm going on my coffee break," Jan said. "Who wants to go with me?"

"You can go on home now," Nurse Cory said to the exhausted man from across the room.

"That's *all* you're going to do, give me a milkshake and send me home?"

Jan dashed to her office, looked around, then grabbed the pen she'd found—it had the hospital's name printed on the side. The exhausted man was still in the ER, dressed and standing near the door.

"Here's a little gift from the hospital staff," Jan said, handing him the pen.

The man put the pen into his shirt pocket. "Any instructions, doctor?"

"Eat," said Doctor Peterson, still sewing the slashed man. He stopped stitching for a moment, rolled his head around, then again bent close to a slash that went from shoulder blade to breast bone.

"It's just a flesh wound," Dr. Dempsey said to the man who was run over. "Just a lot of little cuts and scrapes."

"How was my temperature, nurse? Is my blood pressure normal? I think I went into shock."

"You scraped your leg, you didn't have a heart attack." Nurse Cory was stripping the paper sheets from the exhausted man's bed.

"But it took them so long to get there," said the man who was run over. "I started to get so mad, I thought I might blow a fuse or something."

Jan said, "I haven't worn the same outfit twice. And I haven't even started to mix-n-match yet. You're right, I think we could all learn something from listening to each other tonight."

"Hey doc, will this affect my jogging?"

"It could improve your time if you run in front of cars, especially in the fast lane."

"I was mad too!" the slashed man called.

"You'll know what mad is if you don't stop moving around," Dr. Peterson said.

"Do you need me for anything?" Jan asked. Dr. Peterson didn't answer. "I'm free now—does anyone need anything?" she said, louder, over the din of everyone's mouths moving, hands gesturing, phone blinking, instruments flashing. "Hey!" she said, her face tight with a stretched smile, "What can I do to help? Two comforting hands, two understanding ears for sale here!" Everyone was moving away from her—she realized she was slowly moving backwards when her shoulders hit the wall at the far end of the ER. Such a flurry of crucial activity, such important commitment, so many people at once so significantly engrossed, so urgently occupied, so critically busy—tears flooded into her eyes and her throat choked with the immensity of the occasion, the doctors and nurse absorbed with the patients, the patients with the doctors and nurse. Suddenly Jan shouted, "I understand you so well, I'm on your side, I'm right there with you all the way!" She couldn't hear them anymore. But they were all still working. No one turned to stare at her. Her head was ringing. Nurse Cory went to answer the phone. Jan ran from the room with her hands over her ears.

The hospital was quiet in the wee hours. Nobody in a hospital says the quiet is *like death*. The nurse in the ER dozed with her head on the counter. Doctor Peterson went back to his room and went to sleep on the bed. The television was off in the waiting room and no one was waiting there. The main lobby was dark except a small nightlight in the gift shop, making silhouettes out of the straw flower arrangements. The phone hadn't rung for several hours. Jan sat at her desk. She opened the card again—the party invitation. The party was called a *bash*, and there was no RSVP necessary. Her name wasn't on the envelope. No one walked down the hall. Then the air system went off, increasing the silence. The building didn't even creak. No cars drove by outside.

Jan went quietly into the ER without waking Nurse Cory. In a closet she found several scrub suits, the kinds with cords threaded through the waist bands. She took the ropes out of three of the suits and tied the ends together. Back in her office she examined the ceiling. The light fixture was fluorescent, built flush into the ceiling. So she took a nail file from her purse and used it as a screwdriver to remove the handle from a metal supply cabinet. Then she stood on her desk and fastened the handle to the ceiling. It was tedious because the screws didn't want to go into the ceiling panel and Jan's arms got tired. Finally the handle was in place and she tied one end of the cord to it. Then, standing on her chair, she made a large loop in the other end of the rope. The loop was about the size of her face, and it hung level with her eyes, so, standing in the chair, she was looking through the loop toward the open door of her office into the hallway, and, across the hall, the silent emergency room. She stood there a long time. She had to stand very still because the chair was on wheels, but she had learned poise when she prepared for the beauty contest. She leaned forward slightly so her heels wouldn't make holes in the chair's upholstery. Finally she heard footsteps in the hall, getting louder, and a young man walked past the door. Seconds later he came back and poked his head and shoulders into the doorway. Jan looked at him gravely through the loop. In a hospital you should be serious but never *grave*. "Hi," the young man said. "We need some room-change forms at the third station, but I can see you're busy so I'll come back later." He scratched his chin, grinning. "Oh, you know what? There's a typo on your menu for tomorrow, it says potato croaks instead of croquettes. We all *died* laughing. Hey— you're coming to the big costume party next week, aren't you?" He went on down the hall, whistling. Or else it was another siren outside.

1982

A Chicago woman burst into flames and died, the eighth recorded victim of human spontaneous combustion, based on records dating back to the eighteenth century.

The Three Screwdrivers

She answers the door by opening it then walking away before looking at him or saying hello. "You ready?" he says.

"No." She's gone back to the bathroom, then comes out holding a comb and glances at him quickly. "Well, at least it isn't a *date*."

"What's that supposed to mean?"

"Why d'you wear those disco pants?"

"These?" Cal looks at his legs. The material of his pants is thin and shiny, clinging to his hips and butt, flaring at the ankles. "What's wrong with 'em?"

"They're repulsive. We're not going to a *disco*, are we?" She's still in a bathrobe because she hasn't decided what clothes to wear.

"You don't *have* to come with me." He rubs his thick, short beard with both hands.

She goes back to the bathroom to brush her teeth. "D'you think anything will happen?" A trickle of toothpaste runs down her chin.

"Maybe. It's the right kind of place. Things don't just *happen*, though, you've got to make them happen."

"I know that. Is it anything like where Rudy works?"

"Oh, I forgot your latest Mr. Big works in a bar." He puts his fists in his pockets.

"A fancy one, with an expensive restaurant." The toothbrush in her mouth makes her words blurry.

"Then don't expect it to be the same."

"What kind of people will be there?"

"Whadda ya think . . . a club called Macho's."

"Gays?" Then she laughs and sprays toothpaste against the mirror.

"Not many gay bars hire eight-piece bands. You wanna go to a gay bar?"

"Once was enough. It wasn't my idea."

"Whose was it? Rudy's?"

"Shut up. It was before I even knew him." She spits a mouthful of toothpaste into the sink. "If something doesn't happen tonight, I'll go crazy, I swear I will, sitting at home and *thinking*."

"Don't think you're the only one who ever sat at home thinking," he says.

She looks out the bathroom door at him, then goes back to the mirror. He doesn't look very much like he did five years ago when he was seventeen and they lived in the same neighborhood and walked to school together. She remembers being sad a lot in high school and he would try to joke her out of it. Then one time he used a different approach. He said he kissed her in the first place just to make her stop bawling for a minute. She doesn't remember crying, before *or* after, but she has tried to forget that night so they could go on being friends. She doesn't know whether the friendship has steadily gotten easier or more difficult—she needs someone to talk to after her disastrous affairs.

"Well, you could've *done* something, like I am tonight." She rinses her mouth again and spits. "So who'm I gonna find at this place?"

"A lot of sailors go there."

"Wow. Thanks loads."

"A lot of people. I never took a census."

"But I bet you counted all the babes under sixteen."

"Just the ones with long dark hair."

She shakes her head and her hair lands in place. It used to be long, several years ago. After that it was frizzy, but she recently cut the permanent off the ends. Now it's shorter than his. "Good," she says, still staring in the mirror, but not at herself anymore.

"Don't worry." He's looking at a snapshot of her and Rudy which was lying on the kitchen table. "I hope to God you go home with someone else."

"Me too." She goes into her bedroom, then shouts through the door, "Do I need a purse?"

"You'll hafta buy drinks."

"Darn." She takes off her robe and shivers. "Rudy always made me my drinks. He would only let me have three. Screwdrivers." She dresses quickly and comes back into the living room wearing gray slacks and a loose summer top with very thin straps across her shoulders. She's been working in her garden lately and her shoulders are brown. "But I can make one drink last a long time." She rubs lotion on her hands, hesitates, then takes more lotion and rubs it up both arms and shoulders, under the straps. Cal turns away.

"I liked to just sit and watch him work. Everybody liked him the best, of all the bartenders."

Cal is standing with his back to her, looking at his feet, maybe at the flare of his pants hitting his shoes.

"They all talked to him like they knew him, and you know, it gave me this funny feeling in my chest because only I really knew him. Or so I thought." She stands right beside Cal, but he doesn't move. "But I just sat there quietly watching him, then he would come down to where I was sitting for a few moments and lean over the bar and whisper something to me about one of the customers he'd just been talking to, and everyone would know I was with him, even if he never touched me while he was working." She moves in front of Cal and picks up a silver bracelet from the coffee table, puts it on one arm and pushes it all the way up, almost to her armpit, then shakes her arm until it falls back to her wrist. Cal is watching, but she doesn't meet his eyes. "They all told me I was lucky because Rudy was such a great guy. He always laughed, but I said, I know I am." Cal heads for the door and she goes the opposite direction, to get her purse from the couch. "He wouldn't let any dirty-old-men sit next to me. Everyone was loaded. With money, I mean. Rudy hated it. He couldn't wait to finish night school so he could get a job teaching history. He'll be happy to be among all those wholesome high school kids so he won't have to associate with perverts like me." She drops the bracelet back onto the coffee table.

Cal's been holding the doorknob, staring at her. "You finished? Did that help?"

"No. Let's *go*."

It's early and the parking lot is empty. He takes his trumpet case out of the trunk but she hasn't gotten out of the car yet. "C'mon, hurry up."

"Do I hafta go in *now*?"

"Unless you wanna pay the cover charge."

"I don't want it to look like I'm coming *with* you."

"You and me both, baby."

"Good."

"Look," he says, "after we get through that door, you're on your own. I'm not gonna come to your table or even *look* at you. I'll be looking out for myself, and I damn well better not have to worry about getting *you* home."

"Good. Fine with me. I just don't want anyone to think we came together. It'll ruin my chances if they think I'm with the band."

"Yeah, you'll never get that funny feeling in your chest if people know you're here with the skinny trumpet player."

"The one in disco pants, that's for sure."

They stop near the service door where the employees and band members go in. He knocks. "You sure you wanna do this?"

"I have to. I don't have a choice. I'll go crazy otherwise." A waitress opens the door and they go in. "Otherwise I might end up like *you*, moping around, just getting older."

"Thanks. I can always count on you." He joins the other band members, setting up on a small stage. She sits at a table near the back of the room and orders her first screwdriver.

She nurses the drink a long time, sipping it through the plastic straw that's only meant for stirring. Rudy had warned her not to drink through the straw because she would be affected by the alcohol faster, but it probably was one of his bartender wives' tales. She sucks each ice cube, taking turns, letting them all shrink at the same pace, until each is a sliver, then she leaves the glass on the table, leaves her purse on the seat and makes her way toward the stage where the band is still setting up, saying "test" into microphones, twanging metallic notes, moving the drum set around to make room for more amplifiers. Cal is seated at the back of the stage, his trumpet on a floor stand, his legs stretched out in front of himself. He's holding a glass with both hands on his lap, sloshing the contents in circles without spilling over the rim. She goes around the stage and stands on the floor down below Cal's chair.

"When's this damn thing gonna start?"

"What's your hurry?"

"I've already had a drink. Three's my limit."

"What happens after three? You turn into a pumpkin?"

"Rudy told me three was enough."

"Enough for him maybe, so he wouldn't lose control and find himself in bed with you."

"Har-de-har."

Another band member edges past the drums and brings Cal a jigger of tequila and a glass of beer. Cal quickly finishes what's left in his glass, then takes the jigger.

"Hot shot." She turns away while he empties the jigger, but she doesn't go back to her table. She lowers one strap and rubs her shoulder, slowly, examining her skin. "Hope I'm not peeling."

"You're not."

She turns back toward Cal. He's sipping his beer, getting the foam on his beard, then he wipes it away with his palm.

"I guess I'll go fill my glass with water so they'll think I still have a drink," she says.

Cal laughs. She glares at him. "What's so damn funny?"

"Little Miss Sophisticated. And he called you a pervert?"

"Shut *up*. He never really said that. Just that it wasn't right for him to be with me."

"What's the difference? Just an excuse. I think he was gay. Just your luck. A puritanical queer."

"As *if*. If *only* that was it." She starts to walk away, then turns around once more. "What about your excuses, Cal? How long has it been for you—what're you waiting for?"

She picks up her purse and the glass, fills the glass with water in the restroom, then moves to a table even farther from the stage.

When the band finally starts playing, and she estimates there are about fifty people in the club, half of them dancing, none at any of the tables near hers, she orders another screwdriver. She was going to wait longer, but the waitress came over, picked up the glass of water and stood waiting for her to say something.

She watches the Marines and sailors dance with young Mexican girls with exaggerated eye make up. The girls flip their long hair over their shoulders and keep it flying around in back like silky flags while they dance. The men don't have any hair to flip around. The trumpet and saxophone are out of tune. The drums are too loud, but so is the bass, and the lead singer attacks each note flat, then slurps up to find the pitch. Every song sounds the same. She doesn't tap her feet. She plugs one ear and sips her drink, then plugs the other ear and sips a little more, and the drink lasts through the band's first set.

When the band takes its break, pre-recorded top-forty music comes through the speakers, but not as loud as the band was. "Turn it up!" the girls call from the dance floor, but no one does. She guesses there are about 200 people here now. Cal is coming toward her. She doesn't look at him but is aware that he stumbles over a few chairs. "Hey," he says, still ten feet away. There's still no one sitting at any of the tables around hers.

"What now? I thought you weren't going to talk to me—everyone'll think I'm here with you."

He doesn't sit down. "I just wanted to tell you not to sit way back here. Nothing'll happen if you stay back here, it's too far from the action, people just assume you're not interested in dancing or anything."

She leans back in her chair but keeps both hands on her empty glass, tipping it and tapping it on the table. "What d'you care?" She lifts the glass to drain a few remaining drops from it, but even the ice cubes are gone. "I mean, why're *you* so interested? What're you trying to do, be my pimp?"

"Good idea." He sits backwards on a chair, rapping it against her table. She has to catch her glass before it falls. "I wish I could pick out some guy for you and bring him over here. I wanna see it happen. I wanna *watch* you leave with someone."

She stares at her fingers twirling the glass. When she feels the waitress standing beside the table, she wraps her hands around the glass to cover the fact that it's empty. Cal orders a beer and the waitress leaves.

"You've known I've been with lots of guys. You knew I was with Rudy for half a year . . ." She looks up and finds him staring at her.

He says, "But I knew nothing was going on."

"You wish."

"So why'd you break up, huh? What happened, you asked if he had a prick?"

"Shut up. It was more than grab-ass. I keep telling you, he was in this kind-of church . . ."

"What were the commandments? He couldn't lay any pipe til you converted? Why didn't you?"

"He might've married me if I had."

"Why *didn't* you?"

"It was . . . I wanted him to see . . . we could've been okay together, without that. We could've . . ."

"You *are* a pervert." He stands, laughing. "Trying to seduce a man away from church. Have you no decency?"

"It was a weird church, they didn't even call it church . . . But at least I'm not as wretched as *you*."

"*You* wish." He turns and walks back toward the stage, stops several tables away, then starts to come back, almost shouting over the music, "You're crazy if you think I've gone this long without wetting my wick."

"You bragging or complaining?"

The top-forty music fades out, so Cal runs toward the stage. She picks up her purse, takes a leak in the restroom, then crosses the room and sits at a different table, this one in the middle of a lot of other crowded, noisy tables. There are several empty glasses at her new table, and an ashtray full of cigarette butts. She lays her head on the table for a second, but the smell of the cigarettes makes her even more dizzy. She never felt this way at Rudy's bar. She always remained alert and perceptive, keeping her eyes on Rudy as he laughed with the customers. His teeth were so white. The cocktail waitress used to tell her how fair Rudy was with his tips, sharing with the waitresses and busboys. "Everyone else tries to cheat you all the time," the girl had said. Rudy's fingers never even touched the waitress's hand when he took change from her or handed her the drinks she needed. She lays her head on the table again, then sits up, then props her face up with her hands. Halfway through the set someone asks her to dance. She stares at him. The guy shrugs and moves on to the next table. A very young blond girl agrees to dance with him. A waitress is picking up all the empty glasses from the table.

"Screwdriver," she says, before the waitress asks if she wants anything.

Maybe she slept through the rest of the second set. She doesn't think so, but has a suddenly-woken-up feeling when the band stops playing. Everyone seems to be talking very loud, then they realize they don't have to anymore, and the throbbing conversation settles.

It's the band's table. The lead singer sits across from her. She stares at him, trying to figure out where she's seen him before. A waitress is waiting to get everyone's order. They're all having beer and tequila. She holds her glass, still half full of her third screwdriver, so the waitress won't take it away. Cal lifts one of her drooping straps and puts it back on her shoulder, then sits beside her.

"What're you doing here?" he asks. "Why didn't you dance with that guy?"

"I dunno. He didn't give me a chance to answer."

Cal smokes and drinks. She remembers once when Rudy used his dinner break to bring her home. He'd left her at her door and said, Go to bed,

I'll see you tomorrow. Sometimes he dropped her off and waited in the car until she got into the apartment, but that time he came to the door.

The sax player sits in the last empty seat, on her other side. He has a reed in his mouth instead of a cigarette, then he crushes the reed in the ashtray and everyone at the table cheers. He's wearing jeans, a white shirt and a thin red tie.

She leans toward Cal. "Can I tell you something personal?"

"I can't stop you, can I?"

She giggles. "I mean, I hate your pants. I knew I could tell you, though, I mean, I figured you'd wanna know. What're friends for?"

"Good question."

"But it's a two-way street, y'know. You can tell me something personal now. C'mon, ask me anything. Wanna know what Rudy and I use'ta do at his house?"

Cal puts his cigarette out. She uses her straw to blow the smoke away from her face.

"Okay," he says, "why *did* you go to that gay club?"

The smoke is still bothering her. "A girl at work thought it would solve my problems." She rubs her eyes. "I'd jus' had another two-week disaster with some guy."

"So she thought you should be boffing women instead?"

"I don't think a girl can *boff* another girl."

"Whaddya think lezzies do together, sing campfire songs?"

"No, I jus' mean it's not, like . . . *boff* sounds so hard, like a fight or something. With girls it's . . . softer."

"How'd *you* know?"

"I'm a girl."

"That doesn't mean . . . it can be soft with a guy."

"Didja hear what you jus' said? Bragging about being *soft*?"

"You know I meant it different." He finishes his beer. The waitress is already bringing him another. "That really is a good question," he says, "What're friends for."

"Yeah. A miracle we've been friends so long."

"Have we?"

"Haven't we?"

He drums on the table with his fingers. "Except that night when we were more than friends."

"That night?" She smiles. "We were less than friends. Why doncha wear jeans or something?"

"I don't care what you think of my pants."

"Well . . . if you were wondering why you never score—"

"It has nothing to do with my pants."

"Okay." She closes her eyes and swallows. Her head feels like a brick balancing on a toothpick. She smiles a little and plans to say that to Cal, next time she feels like talking. His breath smells of tobacco and liquor. She opens her eyes and blinks at him. He looks serious and exhausted, but she suppresses her giggle by finishing her screwdriver, draining her glass through the straw.

He says, "We already established your love life isn't a raging success either."

She pushes her glass away, stacks her fists end-to-end on the table and rests her forehead on the top fist. "I know. That much I know. He wouldn't even hold my hand in public. His church, or whatever it was, said it was a sin to be with someone worldly. Anyone not in this church-thing was worldly. But once I was in a theater lobby reading a poster and he came out of the restroom and put his hand on the back of my neck, under my hair . . . God, I had chills."

"Like this?" Cal slides his hand up her neck, but her hair's a lot shorter now.

"No." But she doesn't remove his hand. He strokes her neck like a pet rabbit. "This is weird," she says.

"What I'm doing?"

"No. But I think Rudy was making my screwdrivers a little weaker than these."

"What was a churchy-man doing as a *bar*tender?"

"It was where he worked."

"You sure he put *any*thing in your drinks?"

"Maybe not." Her fists collapse and her head falls to the tabletop. Everyone's drinks jump. "But at least they were free. Beggars can't be choosers!" She can hear the other band members talking but she can't tell how many different conversations. She thinks she's still laughing at the last thing she said, but she's also drooling on her arm. Cal slides his hand onto the back of her head, grasps a fistful of hair, then uses both hands to lift her head and kiss her. She leans against him. He smells of old sweat and cigarette smoke. He lowers one of her straps and groans as he presses his open mouth on her shoulder. She smiles. He pushes the other strap off also, while she's replacing the first one. His mouth moves up her neck, buzzing against her when he says, "I don't want to be doing this. Why am

I?" She opens her mouth as he kisses her again. The beer has washed most of the cigarette taste from his mouth.

"It must be the booze," she laughs, holding onto the table with one arm for balance because he's pulling her out of her chair.

He sweeps both her straps off her shoulders at the same time, and she catches her blouse before it falls. His hands slide over her bare shoulders and down her arms.

"That's what Rudy said once when . . . things started to . . . get going, so to speak. I'd stayed at the bar till he was off, then he had a drink. When he kissed me, when he unbuttoned my shirt . . . he blamed the booze. A very flattering thing for him to say, doncha think?"

Cal groans, his face against her neck, his hands under her blouse, moving up her back. "Oh baby," he bites her earlobe, "Shut up." He takes his hands out of her blouse, holds her head and kisses her again, then kisses her cheek, one eye, and her temple, holding her face next to his.

"But'cha know what?" she says. "I always seem to find the guys who give me just the opposite of what I want at the time."

His mouth is against her ear and he's whispering but it sounds very loud. "Listen, baby," he licks her ear, "you know I was always ready to give you what he wouldn't." He puts his tongue in her ear again, and she laughs.

"But did you ever stop to think I didn't want it from *you*?" She lifts her head so he can kiss her throat.

"You made it pretty clear." He holds her neck in both hands and strokes her cheeks with his thumbs. "But why? Just what the hell did you want?"

"I dunno."

They look at each other. "Have you figured it out yet?"

"Maybe. I dunno. Maybe not."

He pulls her close again, and her chair tilts then almost falls over. Someone is laughing. "Showtime." It's the lead singer. "Save some for later, man." All the band members are finishing their beer and leaving the table. Cal groans and stands.

The waitress begins collecting the empty glasses, then asks if she wants anything. "I dunno." She lays her head on the table and the waitress leaves.

The dance floor is packed during the last set. The girls shriek and the men shout out the words of the songs. They stomp their feet and move faster than the tempo of the music. Many of them dance with beer mugs in one hand. The speakers and the dancing feet make the whole room rattle so the tables actually shake and her head vibrates, along with the ashtray and a few pennies left scattered near the edge. One falls and she watches it roll away. It seems to roll slowly, for a long time, in a wavy line . . . maybe it'll go straight across the dance floor and out the door, across the parking lot—

She sits up. Cal is standing behind her chair. "How're you doing?" He puts his hands on her shoulders. The lead singer is making an announcement, his voice boomy and incoherent. "C'mon, I asked him to play something with no trumpet so we could dance."

"No . . . everyone'll think I'm here with you." She turns and leans against him. His shirt is slippery nylon.

"C'mon."

The band is playing a love song for middle-agers. The dancing couples stand pressed together, rocking back and forth. Cal holds onto her wrist and tightens one arm around her shoulders, working his way to a clear spot on the dance floor, right below the stage. The loudest part of the song is the bass. She practically stands on Cal's feet and holds onto him while he does all the dancing. The song is "After the Loving." She always imagined housewives listening to it play on their kitchen radios, pressing their hands together and closing their eyes. She giggles, and Cal says, "What?"

"Nothing. Never mind."

The band holds out the last chord, a long shimmering out-of-tune noise. The dancers clap, but Cal doesn't move. Groaning again, he says something, but she can't hear him over the cheering crowd as the next song starts. Cal jumps onto the stage.

Either it's the last song or it takes her a long time to get off the dance floor and back to the table, but by the time she gets there, the sax player is already sitting on his instrument case drinking a beer, the drummer lighting a cigarette, Cal holding her purse and looking around nervously. As she approaches the table, his face relaxes and she moves into his embrace. "I was afraid you'd gone home with someone else," he murmurs.

"Don't remind me what a failure I am." Her words are muffled against his shoulder.

"Huh? I didn't hear you."

"Oh well . . . who cares anyway?"

His eyes look weak and tired. "Girl, don't say stuff like that anymore." He picks up his trumpet case but keeps one arm around her as they head for the exit, then he puts his mouth against her head and mumbles into her hair, "What should we do about this?"

"*This?*"

"You know, what're we gonna do now?" He opens the door and the air is surprisingly cool on her face and shoulders. She shivers. The breeze is slightly salty and a low fog is drifting in from the coast.

They stop at the car. "*Now?*" she says. "Now I guess we go home."

He unlocks her door and as soon as she falls into her seat he's pulling her halfway across the stick shift, kissing her throat, her ears, her mouth. She relaxes in his arms, parts her lips, closes her eyes. "Oh baby," his mouth is against her temple, "why don't we move somewhere else. Some small town. I could teach music. You could . . . It would be . . . Oh damn . . ." He pulls her over the stick shift into his lap, slips her blouse down to her waist, moans and touches her breasts. "Oh god, I love you, I love . . ." His hands are shaking. "Let's go away together and start over, forget everything else, oh please, I love you . . ."

She pulls her blouse up and hits her head on the ceiling of the car as she sits upright, straddling the gearshift. Then she moves back over to the passenger seat. "Let's go home, okay?"

"Wha's wrong? You feeling sick?"

"No. Yes. I dunno."

"Hey, wha's wrong? Did I do something wrong?"

She sighs, looking at her feet, in sandals, her toenails painted pink. "I wanna go home and wake up yesterday morning so I can change my mind when you come to pick me up." In the sudden silence, the car begins to feel too warm.

"You mean, that's *it?*"

She doesn't look at him, doesn't move except to wiggle her toes, her voice steady enough but suddenly very weak. "No one ever said stuff like that to me. I wish you were someone else. Why couldn't you be *anyone* else." Sweat trickles down her temples. "Let's just go."

While he drives she pulls her feet up, wraps her arms around her shins and lays her forehead on her knees. Usually riding like this would make her carsick. She never gets sick while driving, so sometimes Rudy would let her drive his sport scar, saying "Slow down!" whenever she went over the speed limit.

Cal pulls up to the curb a few doors down from her apartment, reaching for her while he sets the brake. She already has the door open. Hesitates, then looks at him. "Bye, Cal."

"Wait, can't I come in? I won't . . . Please, can't I just come in and stay . . . ?"

As she starts to get out, he catches her wrist. He's lying sideways across the gearshift halfway into the passenger seat, still holding her wrist as she stands on the sidewalk. Then she yanks her hand away. "Go home, Cal."

She's never seen her neighborhood when it's this quiet. She can hear her footsteps hurrying down the sidewalk and Cal scrambling out of the car, slamming the door. He walks behind her saying, "Please ... *please* ..." She doesn't turn around until she has her door unlocked and she's inside. Cal stands on the porch. She can see the erection in his pants. She looks down, waiting to get sick, wanting to laugh. He leans against the doorway. "I'm sorry," she says, and shuts the door.

She's sunbathing in a bikini before noon on the patio, a book over her eyes, ignoring the phone. It rang at eight, then again around ten. She's watching the time so she can call Rudy at one, if she gets up enough nerve. She is alert and not drowsy and can hear Cal clear his throat before he's within twenty feet of her. Her heart starts beating heavily, but she doesn't move. "Imagine meeting you here," she says, and he clears his throat again.

"I wanted to make sure you were okay."

She sits up and reaches for her robe, but he's staring at her garden. "I wasn't that drunk."

"Oh." He kicks a pebble. He's wearing blue tennis shoes. "But maybe I was drunker than I thought."

"Oh?" She sits in the shade after tying her robe around her waist.

"Yeah." The neighborhood is pretty quiet this morning too, except the birds, lots of them, squawking and singing. "But don't worry about it or think that we can't even be friends anymore," he says, "Cause ... I didn't mean it."

"Didn't mean what?" She shivers. The shade is a lot cooler than the sunshine.

"You know."

He puts his fists in the pockets of his jeans. Their eyes only meet once, then they look away again.

1983

George H. W. Bush broke a Senate tie with his vote to resume the production of nerve gas.

Another Honeymoon Over

They're crossing the desert in late summer. Ranching towns at the foot-hills of the mountains are spaced almost exactly fifty miles apart. The sidewalks seem full of people. Ranchers come into town on Friday night and vacationers stop here before going on to the high Sierra for camping, fishing, cliff climbing, sometimes death—not too often. Wilderness per-mits are issued at the local ranger station. There's a crowd there now as closing time before the weekend approaches.

Tom and Hale have arrived for a chess tournament. Hale drives with one hand and doesn't seem to use his rear-view mirror. The mirror is askew and Tom, in the passenger seat, can see himself in it. His eyes are wide and round. He tries to scowl.

"How was the honeymoon?" Tom asks.

Hale scratches his face. His beard is three days old. "Oh, you know. Married in red, wish yourself dead."

"What's that supposed to mean?"

"I don't know."

"Really, how was it?"

"You don't need me to tell you how things are anymore."

The small-town setting will provide superb conditions for the intense concentration required at a tournament. When Hale was sixteen and Tom seven, Hale taught Tom to play chess. This is the first tournament Hale has gone to since he graduated from college and began teaching woodshop at one of the city high schools, four years ago. When he was ten, Tom started doing yard work to pay for chess lessons. Now he is a nineteen-year-old chess master and people pay him for lessons.

"She's good-looking," Tom says. "You don't mind me saying that, do you?"

"Why should I mind?"

"In that case, she's a *babe*. But also she's got class. You're lucky. No, it probably wasn't luck at all. I hope I find a girl like her, but that *would* be luck."

"Stop talking like a kid, Tommy."

"Isn't it normal to see another guy's girl—sorry, *wife*—and hope I can do as well?"

"Listen, Tommy, from now on our ages will get closer and closer together. People reach a certain plateau and level off, so it seems like they're the same age, okay? Now that you're in the same age group as me, I don't have to be an example to you anymore, okay?"

"Come on, what're you talking about?"

"You know."

They have reservations at the Portal Motel. A painting of a mountain range outlined in neon lights marks the driveway entrance.

"Why a portal?" Tom asks the clerk.

"The Whitney Portal, the start of the Whitney trail. What're you here for anyway?"

"The chess tournament."

"Come on." Hale takes Tom's arm and pulls him away.

The room has two double beds. Hale stretches out on one. Tom does the same. They are the same height and both have the type of blond hair that darkens with age. Hale's eyes are narrow and deep set. On the opposite wall there is a small desk or make-up table and attached mirror. Tom says, "Are you going to call Patty?"

"What for?"

"Don't you remember? This is your one-month anniversary."

"She doesn't expect me to call." Hale gets up, goes to the window and looks out into the parking lot. A motor home is filling up with gas across the street. A woman in blue shorts and sandals comes out of the restroom and gets into the passenger side of the cab. She begins folding a map. "Christ," Hale says. Tom sits up and reaches for his overnight bag. He takes out his handmade portable chess set. The pieces are dark mahogany and light maple, the pawns only an inch high, intricately turned, one by one, on a lathe.

"Why doncha get one of those chess computers?" Hale asks.

"I'm waiting til they're better, til they can beat a grandmaster. What's the use playing something you can kill every time?"

"Then why d'you always want to play me?" Hale says. "Let's go eat."

Tom leaves the chess set on the bed with just the two kings standing in their starting positions.

The air outside is dry and thin and very warm. Hale squints at the mountains. The sun is already behind them. There's still snow on the peaks. Hale shades his eyes, blinking rapidly.

"It sure has been a long time since we've come to a tournament together," Tom says.

"I guess it has."

"I wanted to finish making my tournament set so I could bring it along this time."

After a moment, Hale says, "How's it coming?"

"Maybe you could come home sometime and help me with it."

"You don't need any help."

"Yes I do. The king and queen look too much alike. Maybe I could come to your school in September and work on it during your classes."

Pushing open the glass door of the cafe, Hale turns and stares at Tom, then goes on in and sits on a stool at the counter. Tom sits next to him and twirls once all the way around. On the wall behind the counter are several clocks for sale—Rhett and Scarlet on black velvet with red roses, and another one that has a butterfly for a second hand.

"Listen, Tommy, when I was your age, I was still making chess *boards*. The easy stuff. You got a head start. The same time I was making *my* first board, you had to start yours."

"Yeah, and mine took three times as long to finish."

"For Chrissake, you were ten years old!" Hale leans over the counter, pulls out two menus from the storage shelf and pushes one at Tom.

"You never had to trash one like I did," Tom says.

Hale stares at the menu. They offer cornbread with a bowl of gravy. Bean du jour. The food is shown in colored drawings, the prices typed on paper and taped below each picture. "Maybe most of mine *should've* been trashed."

A tinny radio is playing behind the counter. Tom is drumming his fingers, then he picks up and inspects his fork and spoon. "How many woodshop teachers do they have at your school?" he asks.

"One."

"Maybe someday they'll need to add one and I can get a job at the same school as you."

"Don't be an idiot. Don't you want to design furniture?"

"I don't think so. Do you ever think about trying that?"

"I wasn't ever good enough."

"How about that poker table you made for Dad? I'll bet you could make all the furniture for your new apartment. Wouldn't Patty like that?"

"Decide what to eat—will you?"

Tom looks down at his menu. "Probably by the time I'm teaching high school, you'll be teaching college."

"Yeah, and I was supposed to be a grandmaster by the time you became a master. I haven't even hardly played for over a year. I—Oh never mind."

"What?"

"Nothing. You wouldn't believe me anyway."

"Sure I would."

Hale doesn't answer. His chin is propped in his hand and his mouth is hidden. the radio plays an advertisement, louder than the music, "... nightly to two a.m. ...." Tom puts his menu down. Hale is looking at the waitress who is serving coffee to someone a few stools down. She bends to get a placemat from behind the counter.

"She's not as good as Patty," Tom says.

Hale doesn't move for a moment, then turns and says, "How do you know," with a crooked smile.

"Very funny."

Hale looks back at the waitress. She glances over and he grins.

"But a fool could tell just by looking," Tom mumbles, lowering his head. The waitress is coming to take their orders.

"Shut up," Hale hisses.

The waitress stands in front of them, across the counter. Tom points to a picture of fried chicken and French fries. Hale asks her what it's like to live in a small town in the desert. What is there to do for fun—just bingo?—or is there any live music, some shit-kicking cowboys? Then he points to where the menu says *Chili—in season*. "Say, when's the chili season around here anyway?"

She laughs and leans across the counter.

After she leaves to get their food, Hale sits as though listening carefully to the song which is buzzing on the radio. Tom draws a chessboard on his paper placemat and begins coloring in the black squares.

The song ends. Tom puts his pen into his shirt pocket. "Hale, how'd you meet Patty? I mean, how'd you start going with her?"

Hale rubs his mouth with one hand. "Shit, I don't know. It just happened." He picks up his butter knife and tests the blade with his thumb. "Why?"

"That's just it . . . I mean, it always seems . . . well, almost like the biggest possible coincidence, pure chance . . . to actually meet the *one* person who's going to think you're hell-on-wheels . . . the odds against it are just too much."

"*What* are you talking about?"

"Remember your first girlfriend—Darla?"

"Not really."

"You brought her in to meet Mom and Dad in the family room. Then when you were leaving, after they couldn't see you anymore, you put your arm around her. I was hiding and watching you, but I couldn't figure out *how* something like that starts. All I could see was you just *started*. You already knew what to do. You *always* knew what to do and when to do it, without asking and without being told."

"I gotta take a leak." Hale stops on his way to the restroom to say something to the waitress. She laughs. There are also toys for sale, on a narrow shelf under the clocks. A highway patrol racing set. The radio plays a whole cowboy ballad before Hale comes back. His hair is damp and his face flushed. "Sure is hot," he says.

"What were you going to say, Hale?"

Hale turns and looks at Tom for a moment. "Nothing."

"I mean before you went to the bathroom."

"Was I going to say something?" He drinks half of his glass of ice water.

"You okay, Hale?"

"Yeah, sure."

Tom waits until Hale finishes his glass of water. "Anyway, compare you and Darla to one of my first dates. When I brought her home, she said her parents weren't there so she was scared to go inside alone."

Hale is looking past Tom, down the counter. Tom turns also, sees the waitress taking two plates from under the hot lights.

"Anyway," Tom says, "I said okay and went in with her." The waitress doesn't linger after putting their plates in front of them. She glances once at Hale. "Well," Tom says, "she said she was still scared and asked me if I would stay until she was in bed. I said okay, so she went down the hall and into her room. I saw her light go on and we talked back and forth a little, then I saw her light go off and she said, Okay I'm in bed now. So you know what I did? I said goodnight and went home. What a dumbshit. Next day, she wouldn't speak to me."

Hale is staring at his hamburger, then slowly begins picking seeds from the bun.

"I'll bet you never had to learn the hard way like that."

"What makes you so sure?"

"You had lots of girls. Maybe that's why you were able to find one like Patty by the time you got married. At the rate I'm going, I'll be forty before I start finding girls as good as her."

"You sound like a dick. Eat and shut up," Hale says.

When the waitress comes by again, Hale holds out his glass for more water.

"Too bad we don't have a liquor license," she says.

"Oh well," he smiles. "I'm sure there're other places in town that serve beer."

Tom doesn't talk while he eats. Hale is holding his water glass with his left hand, but not lifting nor drinking out of it. His arms lie on either side of his plate.

"You okay, Hale?"

"Go on back to the room. I'm going for a little walk to give you a chance to study without distraction."

"I'm just going to review. We could do that together. Aren't you going to review some openings? I'm trying out a new opening tomorrow."

The waitress picks up their plates, smiles quickly, turns the radio off, then moves a few steps away, wiping something with a cloth. Somebody at a booth drops a dish and several men laugh and applaud. Hale dips his little finger into his water glass then puts the finger in his mouth and draws it out silently.

"I didn't really come out here to play chess as much as for a little vacation," Hale says.

"You just had a honeymoon in Coronado!"

Hale scratches his face again. The sound is loud and rough. "I'll be back soon. I have to find out something."

"Can I come with you?"

"No." Hale stands, walks toward the exit, then stops and turns around again. Tom is still on his stool at the counter, but turned, facing the doorway where Hale is standing. His eyes are round. They always made him look as though he were holding his breath.

"Christ," Hale whispers.

He says, "I'll tell you when I get back, Tommy."

The motel room is very warm. Tom turns on the air-conditioner, then lies on the bed with the chess set. The pieces keep rolling under his body. He has to get off the bed to finally find all the pieces and put them back on the board. Then he gets his postal chess notebook and a book of chess openings from his overnight bag. The latest postcard from a postal opponent is marking a page in the book. He looks at the list of game moves in his notebook, then opens the book to the page where the postcard is, looks at the diagram for a long time, then closes the book, picks up the phone and asks to place a collect call to Los Angeles. Patty doesn't answer the phone.

He goes to the small desk and mirror. Sitting down at the desk, he leans forward on his elbows toward the mirror and concentrates on his eyes. Hale has a little muscle that flexes between his eyebrows which pulls the brows together when he is thinking, speaking with intensity, or glaring. Tom has to touch himself between his own eyebrows with an index finger before he can find the muscle and flex it. He practices, watching his eyes glare, and finally tries to hold a glare as long as possible, timing himself.

Hale comes in. "What're you doing?"

"Nothing." Tom quickly leaves the desk and goes back to his bed. He picks up the chess set. None of the pieces have been moved away from their starting positions.

"Want to play a friendly little game tonight? It'll be a good warm-up," Tom says.

"I'm no work-out for you."

"Sure you are!"

"Cut it out, Tommy." Hale scratches his cheek. "You know, you probably play too much chess."

"That's impossible." Tom smiles, but Hale doesn't. "I never have as much time as I want to study, I never seem to understand as much as I'd like to, and sometimes I just can't concentrate—"

"You're crazy, that's what you are. There's not even any real competition for you at this dinky little tournament."

"Sure there is, there's always some competition—"

Hale is staring at Tom's overnight bag.

"What's the matter, Hale, are you okay? If you don't feel like staying, we can go home—"

"Don't you want to know what I found out?"

"Yes."

Hale goes toward the bathroom as he unbuckles his pants. He strips to his boxer shorts, hangs the pants on a hanger on the bathroom door. "There's a sort-of nightclub in this town, a guaranteed place. I asked around." He takes off his shirt.

"Guaranteed for what?"

"Don't be such a baby." Then Hale smiles without showing any teeth. "It's got what you want, buddy. You can't miss."

Tom can't find the muscle he was using to make the glare. He glances in the mirror. "No thanks."

"Why not! Hey, Tommy, think of it this way: a place like this is more honest. No one is pretending that they're out shopping or getting a suntan when they're actually looking for something else."

"Did you find Patty like that?"

Hale whirls from the sink. His face is wet. Then he picks up a towel and takes a long time to dry.

"I'll look up the address of this club," Hale finally says, dropping the towel on the floor. "It can't be far. *Nothing's* that far away in this place. I'll drive you over."

"Wait a second—you can't just *leave* me there. Even if I . . . meet someone, where would I take her!"

"To *her* place, man! If she doesn't have her own place, she'll make arrangements. If she couldn't make arrangements, she wouldn't be there."

Tom sits cross-legged on his bed, holding the chess set in his lap. He looks at each of the white pawns in order. "I don't really feel like it."

"How does your prick feel about it?"

Tom looks up.

"You said you're worried about your concentration. Well, here's a way to improve it." Hale lies on his bed, his hands under his head, his biceps bulging and knotty. "You just wait and see how well *I* play tomorrow!"

A television is on in the next room and someone laughs. Tom picks microscopic motes of dust from his chess board. He opens his mouth, slowly pulls his lower lip over his teeth and bites down. Hale chuckles softly. "Hell, I'll be so relaxed, maybe I'll even beat *you* tomorrow." Tom looks up. Now Hale is watching him closely. The hair on Hale's chest is dark with dampness, and the hair on his forearms and the backs of his hands—also wet and dark. Tom puts the chess set down on the mattress. He stands up on the bed, his head nearly to the ceiling. Hale jumps up too, on his own bed. The mattresses groan. Tom kicks the chess set. The pieces spray against the wall like buckshot. Tom leaps off the bed, Hale coming after him.

Tom's head is pinned to the wall, Hale's forearm braced under his chin. Tom's eyes no longer round. "Stupid little shit," Hale says. They breathe hard, looking at each other.

1984

A twelve-day-old baby, born with a cardiac malformation, lived for three weeks with a baboon heart.

Each Other's History

During the previous two decades:

The summer Olympics dominated her dad's black-and-white TV for two weeks the beginning of the election season. She has a vague but persistent memory of the phrase "running for president" in a news-anchor voice-over, while the distorted B&W screen showed an Olympic track. She believed Nixon and Kennedy were running around that track to see who would be president. Kennedy had funny hair. Nixon's was more like their father's, combed straight back from a curved, receding hairline. But she knew their father's hair was not exactly like Nixon's, because once on a long car trip, she had imbecilicly asked her mother, "what color is dad's hair?"

"Blue," her mother shot over the back seat, then turned back around.

"His hair is so dark blue that it looks black," her sister explained in a hushed voice. The explanation made sufficient sense, so the illogic of having blue hair never troubled her.

So the one with funny hair won the race, the Cuban missile crisis passed without touching her cognizance, three years later the man who'd run the fastest was shot, followed by interminable spooky days thick with the despondent preoccupation of every adult, the funeral procession plodded as though through glue through an endless weekend afternoon, wiping out all the cartoon shows she might've watched in black-and-white, swearing she was seeing the red of Popeye's kerchief.

She got a Brownie camera for her eighth birthday but her mother would only let her use black-and-white film because color developing was too expensive. She took the requisite pictures of The Grand Canyon, The Old Man in the Mountain, Half Dome, and the White House, during another infinite car trip, this time in a camper without her father's head always in her field of vision so she needn't ponder the color of his hair, and anyway was old enough to know better. Her black-and-white photos of The Washington Monument and Old Faithful were remarkably similar.

When she was eleven she got a paper route, then let her younger brother come along on Sunday mornings. He and she both received their first fishing poles and reels the same Christmas. So it wasn't unusual their baseball mitts were also the same age, his with Maury Wills' signature and hers had Brooks Robinson's. They played catch, both of them pitchers, winging fastballs in at each other, or one would bounce grounders for the other to field then throw a frozen rope to first. But when he suited up for baseball games on the dirt fields behind the junior high, she remained in the bleachers, legs spread and feet propped up, smacking a fist in her mitt, ruminating on whatever phenomenon might cause the coach to spot her and call her down to the field, to the pitching mound or batter's box, to save the game, to be the first girl to be allowed to play Little League.

Consolation did arrive. The San Diego Padres, in their first year as a Major League franchise, may not have acknowledged girls when they held paperboy night at the stadium, but girls could be Junior Padres. So she was invited to join the Junior Padres when her brother's Little League team sent in their 7-Up bottle caps. They each received six free games and a Padres t-shirt—a thin undershirt with a silk-screened logo, which she persistently wore, even after it began to stretch unbecomingly over her developing body.

Of course baseball clubs have reasons for courting kids, *all* kids: While developing future players in the minor leagues, Major League clubs develop future fans with a festival atmosphere and giveaways, trying out everything to see what's going to succeed: the free t-shirts and caps and balls and posters, "the wave" surging through the crowd, the cotton candy and (later) nachos and (even later) sushi, the beach balls batted around overhead. Or maybe even the players and the game itself. For her, nearly overnight twenty-five men between the ages of twenty and forty playing a mythical, aesthetically symmetrical game became more important, even more genuine than any of the beardless faces in the crowd at a junior high party who might (but never did) ask her to dance.

She tried to take pictures of them, the players—catching, swinging, running. But the Brownie was out of its league and only produced images of the backs of her brother's teammates' heads and a whitish blur beyond them. The first fly ball she witnessed from the top of the upper deck caused her a gasp of astonishment at how far the ball was hit, the towering elegant arc of it, yet still it didn't even count—was just a useless *out*.

Minor league ballplayers call the big leagues "The Show." In 1969 the former minor-league Padres entered The Show as an expansion team full of rookies nobody wanted and castoffs too used-up to play for a contender. Names like Ed Spezio, Ivan Murrell, Chris Cannizzaro, Al Ferrara, Al Santorini, Al McBean, and Billy McCool. They owned Joe Neikro, not at the end of his career, but the beginning. And the Padres had another pitcher named Johnny Podres. Between January 1, 1969, and the start of the season, no fewer than ten boy babies were born who would someday become players on the Padres. The boys old enough to play in 1969, and those a little too old, won 51 games and lost 110. San Diego was not a young city but an old one, 200 years in 1969, the year Major League Baseball turned 100.

Those who call themselves purists decry baseball in San Diego as being without tradition, without the character born of a long and colorful history dotted with triumphs, controversy, curses, rivalries and disappointment. But when you follow a team from the time you're eleven, you don't care that it has no history before you—you and the team evolve together. And in many ways, you are each other's history.

In 1970, even though she was unaware that the mayor and several city council members were indicted for corruption, she knew that the Padres manager committed the unforgettable (and unforgotten) crime of pulling his starting pitcher in the eighth inning of a no-hitter he was losing 0–1. In 1972 she didn't have a new camera yet, but finally had her own transistor radio. She didn't miss a single game broadcast that year. Some of the names were new: Johnny Grubb, Leron Lee, and Enzo Hernandez (shortest player in the league, fewest RBI for anyone with 500 at-bats, and acquired in a trade that sent a future twenty-game-winner to Baltimore). She wasn't aware that the Republican National Convention was scheduled to occur in San Diego that summer and at the last minute was moved to Miami to thwart protestors; or that in the public-relations fallout the mayor announced a week-long celebration for San Diego as "America's Finest City," and the name stuck. She remembers the catchphrase— it was used for decades afterwards—but assumed the city had won it in a contest. She was, however, entirely aware that Nate Colbert made baseball history when he hit five home runs and batted-in thirteen in a doubleheader. She clipped every article and photo in the newspaper after a winning game and pasted them in a handmade scrapbook. She bought (and actually chewed the gum inside) packs of Topps baseball cards, searching for any of the Padres. For one glorious day she lay on the sand at Torrey Pines beach—while her brother frolicked and her sister read college books—and listened as the Padres climbed out of last place for the first time in their Major League history

Although she had no cognizance of Title IX, she could've participated in high school softball, could've learned the importance is in being a cog in the wheel, being a part that makes up a whole. But she saw what girls were wearing—just their usual PE clothes that their parents had to buy anyway—as opposed to the boys' complete home and road uniforms, with high-cut stirrup socks and white sweatshirts with red sleeves under button-up jerseys, *Matadors* on the white home uniform, *Mt. Miguel* on the grey visitors. Saw the dirt field the girls were given, as opposed to the boys' green, mowed grass. Saw the army duffel bag of scuffed bats and balls the women's coach dragged out to the dirt field, and the beat-up, flat canvass bases that didn't fasten to the ground. Mostly saw how the huge softball didn't fit her Brooks Robinson mitt, and didn't even try out.

If it were just sports she wanted, she could've gone for track, still a constituent of a team, but also striving as an individual, school records, league records, state records to be broken. But it wasn't that. It was the way everything stood absolutely stone-still, a frozen image; then, first, the pitcher moved, and the uncoiling of his body—from slow stretch to powerful acceleration to discharge—was like the proverbial butterfly who sneezes halfway around the world and a hurricane begins: After the pitcher unfurls, the batter, swinging, is the second release of the loaded spring. Then the swirl of momentum expands. The batter is propelled, by the pitcher's wind-up and the swing of his own bat, into a wider orbit around the infield; second baseman and shortstop surge in synchronization to cover bases or line up to cut off a throw-to-home; third and first basemen dash in or move sideways, outfielders in the far-reaches of the current swirl left or flow right; until the whirlpool centralizes again, the vortex is a collision play at third base or a slide into home.

For Christmas she wished for a new camera, and received her grandfather's Pentax with a mirrored viewfinder that you had to look down into, holding the camera at waist-level. Looking into a tiny mirror, it was difficult to move the camera quickly and keep it centered on moving objects.

She got stack after stack of smears, maybe a foot or back of a head recognizable. She stuck with black-and-white, even though color developing was becoming the norm and it now actually took longer for the drug store to develop her B&W blurs than if they were color. But discovered the school journalism class had cameras to borrow, and a darkroom, so she signed up for summer school photography, and the next fall was a photographer for the school paper.

In the meantime she spent hours pitching a baseball against a brick wall beside the driveway, counting balls and strikes or fielding the resulting grounder or line drive, keeping track of hits, outs and runs in her head, until a nine inning game was over and she was the winning pitcher. By this time Johnny Podres was long retired and a young staff was actually allowing the Padres to lose by scores of 1—0 or 2—1 instead of 8—2 or 15—5. There was a dentist who had a private practice and came two outs from throwing a no-hitter. There was a screwball specialist not even six feet tall. And her icon, Clay "The Kid" Kirby, someone's handsome hometown hero pitching in the Major Leagues, losing twenty games but sustaining an ERA under three. In 1970 and 1971 he'd had no fewer than three near no-hitters—he was the one who earned infamy when his manager pinch-hit for him in the eighth inning of one of them, then he lost two others for lack of run support. For all the stale Topps gum she chewed, she never got one of his baseball cards to prop against her radio, but it was his pitching motion she memorized and practiced from her pitching rubber (a crack in the front walk); and it was his teammate that she fantasized herself becoming. But who would discover her, how would this come about? Would scouts spot her pitching against a backstop at the local elementary? Would she win a raffle to pitch an inning and prevail so well they couldn't let her go? Or perhaps she would catch the eye of her young hero whose instant ardor would lead him not to ask her to a drive-in movie or grasp her breast, but to invite her to train with him.

During a time she didn't know why she wasn't feeling the surging hormones her health class predicted would arise, it was comforting to understand the infield fly rule or how the conditions are right for the hit-and-run. When she had no idea how her body could ever want another person to penetrate her with a part of himself, it was easier to yearn for Clay Kirby or Dave Roberts to strike out Pete Rose two times in a game. It was preferable to be anxious and apprehensive only because of the batters' consistent impotence to produce runs for these endowed young pitchers, rather than agitate about why boys didn't call her on the phone or what would she do if one ever did. When she had only a vague idea what was involved when girls spoke of *making out*, but also had no desire to find out, it was condoling to find out there were at least eight ways for a runner to score from third with less than two outs and that, until his Achilles snapped, Dave Campbell could be counted on for any one of them. And then when the other school-newspaper photographers practiced for their future dates with real girlfriends by approaching her from behind—while she developed photos in the darkroom—to cup and squeeze her breasts, she forgot to stew about it alone at home. For at least two hours she was busy listening to Jerry Coleman give personality to each futile ground ball or lonely two-out hit or impudent and costly error. For two hours too consumed with concern about Fred Kendall's alarmingly low percentage throwing out runners attempting to steal to worry about the circumstances at school she'd allowed to continue with boys she actually viewed as her friends. The darkroom was dark, and she seldom turned around, so she was never positive which boy it was. When they did eventually get girlfriends, the squeezing went on for a while, until (most likely) the girlfriends finally let the boys touch *their* breasts, so the boys no longer needed the shadowy, amber-lit, taciturn darkroom groping. And within weeks, the girlfriends had asked their boyfriends not to be in the darkroom when she was also there, or even be friends with her anymore.

With that going on, how could she have any knowledge about C. Arnhold Smith, the Padres owner. That he'd once been named "Mr. San Diego," that he controlled a taxicab/hotel/tuna fleet/real estate/banking/ brokerage empire; that he was an insider crony of Richard Nixon's and laundered hundreds of thousands of dollars in campaign funds for him; that other Nixon insiders shielded him from federal banking regulators; that his bank was making defaulted loans to mob-connected companies, some owned by Smith himself; that Nixon's fall spelled the undoing of Smith's fortune and as Nixon's power dissipated, auditors swarmed into C. Arnhold's bank and discovered it had been looted; that despite billions of dollars of deposits, Smith's bank collapsed in fall of 1973, at the time the biggest bank failure in U.S. history. What she *was* acutely aware of, in January of 1974, was that the Padres, after six losing seasons and some nights with only 2,000 people in the 60,000-seat stadium, had their moving vans packed and would be leaving in the morning for a new home in Washington DC. Then, mere hours before departure—after she, having just turned eighteen, had agitated herself to sleep—McDonald's Hamburgers baron Ray Kroc bought the team and ordered the vans unpacked.

During the rest of the '70s, when first Randy Jones then Gaylord Perry won the Cy Young Award in Padre uniforms, boys once again touched her in the darkroom. They were different boys in a different darkroom. They were supposed to be called men. She was in college.

Dave Winfield was a college man who went straight to the Major Leagues, not riding the bench or pinch hitting, but playing regular, and hitting too. Unfortunately Clay Kirby was gone by then, traded away for more hitting, the hitting he had always needed, straight from O'Henry, traded away to get it.

Other players came and went during the Dave Winfield era. Even some whose names were familiar from other, better, parts of their careers. Willie McCovey, Bobby Tolan, Tito Fuentes, Doug Rader, Willie Davis. A few, like Ozzie Smith, would go elsewhere for greatness. Still, there were the likes of Mike Champion, Tucker Ashford, Rick Sweet, Paul Dade, and a catcher who developed a neurosis about throwing back to the pitcher. At times Winfield seemed a powerful Gulliver playing a boys' game with bumbling gnomes.

When *Fear of Flying* was on the list of supplementary reading for her American lit survey class (and she read it ten times instead of any of the regular class books by Hemingway, Fitzgerald, Steinbeck, Salinger, Faulkner, Updike or Malamud), *Ball Four* was the other book she read that year, and read that one ten times as well. The spines of both books disintegrated, and she held them together with rubber bands.

She happened to wear a dress to school. Once. Wondering if anything would be different. That day when a young man came up behind her in the darkroom—as she stood at her enlarger booth, dodging and burning a print she was exposing—he put his hands up under her skirt, pushed her underwear aside, put his fingers inside her . . . laughed.

Another time, once—on her way from the darkroom to the basketball gym, as she was passing the temporary office trailer parked in the quad with "Answers" printed on its side—she climbed the portable metal steps and went inside, to the walk-in counseling clinic. Once. Of course, the counselor—who might have been twenty-five and wore one bandanna wrapped around her head, another tied at her throat, and still another tied around the thigh of her frayed jeans, a sheer peasant blouse, and sandals—asked what was bothering her, but she couldn't make words that were a reasonable answer. *The Padres have been all-pitching and no-hitting for seven years* wasn't anything to go to a counselor for. So she didn't mention the Padres or baseball when the counselor asked about her major, her career plans, her hobbies. Then the counselor said, So, you probably came from a high school where you knew everyone and everyone knew you, and now you're anonymous at the big, cold, indifferent, university.

She said she didn't think she minded that part.

The counselor said, You need to find a core of people who know you, and you know them, and you all care about the same things. That's the first step toward caring about each other. People who care about each are never alone.

She said she didn't mind doing things alone.

The counselor said, Maybe there's a photography club you could join.

She said she was probably already in something like that.

The counselor said, Can you become more active there? Maybe volunteer for something, that's how you meet new people, and they meet you.

She said she took assignments; that's how photography worked.

The counselor said, That sounds like work, and the rest of your life will be work. These years are supposed to be when you reach out, discover, explore, find yourself.

She said that the things that were probably supposed to happen, they weren't happening.

The counselor said, You've got to make things happen. Do something spontaneous.

But all that winter while she crouched with her camera at basketball games wondering why she felt such terror and rage when nothing was happening to her, her brain registered and retained a name repeated over the nearly-empty arena's loud speaker like a mantra, *Assist by Tony Gwynn, assist by Gwynn, field goal Gwynn, another assist for Tony Gwynn.*

She finally figured out that photojournalism wasn't going to cut it. She had no access to the locker rooms and had to do all her shooting from the sidelines. She switched to candids of athletes on the bench, not even sure which one was this Tony Gwynn. Her senior photojournalism project of sweaty athlete faces earned a C.

So what does a photojournalism major do when she gives up on action shots? She began the program to become a secondary school English teacher. There weren't enough positions for high school photography teachers, and an English teacher often was the newspaper advisor anyway.

On September 25, 1978, nearing the end of what should have been Ozzie Smith's Rookie-of-the-Year first season, she left early from her course on the theory and practice of secondary education, in order to arrive on time at the junior high where she would begin her semester there as a student teacher. She would soon discover that seventh graders didn't know the difference between a verb and an adjective. She would in weeks to come stand in front of them singing "I Can't Smile Without You," plugging in the substitute nouns and verbs they'd chosen in a mad-lib game. She would observe how the blossoming girls painted tears on their cheeks with mascara, possibly because they outweighed most of the boys in their classes by fifty pounds and towered over them by as much as a foot. She would have the opportunity to take a knife away from one of those boys no taller than four feet whose lucid brown eyes filled with tears while they walked together to the principal's office.

But that first day, it could've been her eyes filling with tears on the long walk across campus to the parking lot on the southwestern side of campus, lugging a gargantuan camera bag packed, in addition to the camera, with expensive education textbooks—each with a chapter on adolescent psychology. Her first day, and recognition already dawning that she felt no passion, didn't view this a life's calling, was doing it for the wrong reasons.

She saw the smoke as soon as she came from the education classroom. A column of it, she could just see the top of it over the buildings. A fire, she thought, and it hadn't been burning long—it hadn't even started to dissipate at the top of the column. It looked like it might be coming from the parking lot where her car was. A car fire, oil burning. Maybe at the frat houses that flanked the parking lots. The boys (or men) who shouted things at girls walking to their cars. As she approached the parking lot, although more of the monolith of smoke was visible, still not its place of origin or cause. It was farther away than she'd thought. And it was bigger than she'd thought. The smoke was black, and now she could see distinct gusts fuming and unfurling within the column as it continued to grow and billow skyward. The crown was starting to mushroom.

When she entered the southbound freeway, traffic was still moving at a decent speed. The column of smoke, looming huge, was just off to the right. Two, three, four freeway exists in a row had highway patrol cars parked across the lane, red, blue and white lights flashing, officers just now setting up barricades to close the off ramps. Only then did she think to try the radio, set to the Padres broadcast station, which was yakata-

yakata the rest of the day. There was no waiting through advertisements for insurance or Chevrolets, for the best home remodeling or the smoothest golf courses. A near-hysterical news reporter was blithering, ". . . oh, no . . . oh god, bodies everywhere, pieces of bodies . . . the destruction . . . suitcases and pieces of seats, paper flying and still falling, hunks of metal just peeled away, pieces of the wings, so much smoke, oh my . . . oh I've never seen anything like it . . ."

As she continued south past the barricaded ramps, coming north-ward on the other side of the freeway were fire truck after fire truck, ambulance after ambulance, police cars from La Mesa, Chula Vista, National City, the county sheriffs, lights flashing, sirens wailing, veer-ing through traffic that had started to thicken and slow down. They didn't know the toll yet, they didn't know the cause, all they knew was that on a clear, sunny morning, a 727 jet making its approach to Lindbergh Field had struck a Cessna, had literally halted in its vapor trail and plummeted to the ground in a North Park neighborhood, at the time the worst airline crash in U.S. history.

After a semester with just one class at the junior high, she set out to complete her credential with a spring semester of three classes at a high school. Before a month was behind her there, she knew that she would not be seeking employment in secondary schools. Perhaps she stayed anyway because her new supervising teacher paid more attention to her than anyone had since her parents, paid attention to things about her besides her inept attempts to be more interesting than the din always present in the tenth grade classroom. He even wanted to see her photo-graphs, which were still mostly the candids of athletes on the sidelines, on the bench. She hadn't gotten any good ones of anyone in the Padres dugout, although she had tried with a zoom lens from the field level seats, where she had sneaked last season during the eighth and ninth innings of games, when everyone else had already given up and was on their way home. Almost by accident, she'd gotten a nice, shadowy, even ghostly shot of the bat rack. Maybe that was why she'd also started looking for shots in other parts of the stadium: *Padres Suck* graffiti writ-ten on the back of a seat, the hotdog condiment stand with scattered onion and relish and a crime-scene blood smear of ketchup, the golf cart that looked like a giant baseball that used to bring a relief pitcher to the mound but since the gas crisis had been parked on the plaza above the outfield below the scoreboard. Looking at her photos from over her shoulder, from behind her head, the supervisor put his hands on her upper arms. She continued flipping slowly through the stack of prints. Once he said "Hmmm," and his chin or mouth rested for a second on the crown of her head. It was but wasn't like the boys in the darkroom. She had never felt that way before. She didn't want to do anything to move him away, so she didn't do anything. It might have been only a few weeks later, he told her of his marital troubles, of his wife's disinterest in sex. Once they were standing alone together in the teachers' workroom, and one of them said, When does life begin?

Maybe at twenty-three? she said.

Maybe at thirty-one, he said.

They stood looking at each other until she dropped her eyes. She turned away.

The baseball season started just after her supervising teacher seemed to lose all interest in her. Still, Gaylord Perry, Randy Jones, Dave Winfield and Ozzie Smith were promising better than a last-place finish. At the end of the season's first month, and her last month of student teaching, The Padres were 9-14, in fourth place but flirting with third. She finished that term, and sometimes thinks back and calculates where those students would be now. Only four years younger than her, they could be doctors or lawyers or professors or bankers in the upwardly-mobile years of their careers. They could be in jail or dead. But they could also be animal trainers or caterers or disc jockeys or wildlife biologists or sculptors or news anchors or musicians or waitresses . . . or baseball players who'd won eight batting titles . . . or had long since washed-out.

No longer shooting sports for the college newspaper, she enlarged her series on the unseen, unnoticed corners, quirks and eccentricities of baseball fields and stadiums, including some minor league parks within a 200 mile radius, plus college and public athletic fields, even Little League.

But she needed a job, now that college was finished. She needed her own darkroom and needed something to call her life.

One day she went to an inner city neighborhood park to take shots of an old ball-field with concrete bleachers and concessions and even scorekeeper's booth, but when she got there discovered the field, as well as the adjoining fields, were being used for a dog show. Instead of turning around and leaving the parking lot—filled with campers and vans and full sized motor homes—she squeezed into a parking spot that someone had half filled with collapsible pens holding shredded newspaper and squalling puppies. A backstop behind a pen of hounds on home plate might not be a bad shot for her series.

The baseball field had disappeared under a grid made by fluttering surveyor's tape slung between posts pounded into the turf. Each cube of the grid had a shade tarp, and inside the area squared-off by surveyor's tape, people lined up with their dogs while someone in a suit or dressy dress examined them, sometimes touching them, sometimes just looking, sometimes asking them to trot back and forth, each dog individually, then all the dogs at once, before pointing at one of them, and four or five people watching from outside the surveyor's tape would clap, then all the dogs would drain from the square and a new set would come in.

She wandered past squares where the Labs lined up, then golden retrievers, then collies and ones that looked like little collies, poodles of all sizes, beagles and dalmatians. She didn't know the names of most of the others. While she was looking, she noticed: after all the dogs of one kind were finished, and one of them was chosen, the winning dog was posed in the center of the ring, with the judge holding the ribbon, and a photographer showed up. The equipment he was lugging included a shoulder satchel, a sign with slots to change the date and name of the dog show, and a large-format camera. He set up for the shot quickly—no light meters or analysis of the background—then tossed a rattling, fluttering toy up and over his back. As the dog's ears came up and its eyes followed the toy, the photographer took the shot. He took two shots, then wrote the dog's number on a pad, gathered his equipment and hurried off to another ring, another winner.

That day she thought, briefly and for the first time, about the hippie college counselor, while she spontaneously chose two things: her job and her dog. The dog was a clumber spaniel. The slowest, squattiest, ugliest of the spaniels, with droopy red-rimmed eyes and a big wet smile. For agreeing to show the dogs, and in exchange for some promotional photos of the breeder's other dogs, the owner of Quagmire Clumber Spaniels let her buy a chubby, slobbery male puppy, provided she also took a gangling six-month-old bitch, bred her and returned the pick puppy to the breeder.

Getting the dog show superintendent to include her as one of the show photographers didn't take as much agreeing. Another photographer had recently retired. But there was no paycheck, no benefits, it was self-employment, her own business, and she had to figure out fast how to know who was who in which photo, how to bill them, how to keep track of who paid, how much to charge, how to run the fastest when the loud speaker called for a show photographer to such-and-such ring, to get there first and be the one to take the shot.

If she failed, there'd be no one to fire her. No one to give her back her old job. But she was glad that when the Padres decided having their long-time broadcaster as the team's manager hadn't worked, they gave Jerry Coleman back his microphone and headset after another year of sixth place malaise—brightened once or twice by the speedsters who made the Padres the first team to ever have three players stealing fifty or more bases in a season.

The next season was no better, but she was getting the hang of being a dog show photographer and turned a small profit. Her dogs—whom she named Quagmire The Kid Kirby and Quagmire Perfect Game, and weren't anything like the lithe, speedy team the Padres kept thinking they were building—were still too undeveloped to show, but they doggedly padded after her from room to room of her one-bedroom rental house in North Park, not too far from where the jet had crashed, where, in the former one-car garage, she set up her darkroom, not to be used for the color dog show photos but for the continued printing of shots for her evolving book of black-and-white scenes from baseball parks.

Following that season the Padres hired Dick Williams to manage, and 1982 foreshadowed what would soon come about. There was an eleven-game winning streak and a fourth place finish instead of sixth. There was the first cocaine bust and suspension for a swift and cocky second baseman. There was a bona fide .300 average. And, called up from the minor leagues to The Show in mid-season, there was a rookie named Tony Gwynn.

There was also another dog show photographer who suggested they'd do better if they combined into one business. There was her final selected 100 best baseball stadium photos collected into a book proposal. And there was her male clumber, Clay, consistently taking the points, going best-of-winners, then finishing his championship.

She couldn't show her dog herself because she couldn't skip working a show, so she hired a handler, and Clay went on the road. He did so well, he stayed on the road in 1983, partially paying for his handler's fees with stud service, the rest made up with free promotional photos provided for the handler's other dogs.

Tony Gwynn broke his wrist, then came back to hit .348 the last two weeks of the season, but the time off did its damage and his average did not rise above .300. Nobody thought anything about it at the time, but it would never happen again. That season he was still just a platoon player.

It was obvious Clay was more bonded to his handler than to her, but she still had the bitch, Kirby, who followed her everywhere, with heavy, patient, steady footsteps. The bitch hadn't turned out good enough to show. But the dog show photography business was easier combined with the other photographer. He could churn out every photo from a weekend show by Tuesday, and she had them in the mail with billing info by Thursday. He said it would be even easier if they weren't doing it from two houses, so he moved into her one-bedroom house, and they got married in January. It did not seem spontaneous until it happened.

That was the beginning of 1984.

Her male dog who she hadn't seen in over a year was the top ranked clumber in the country, and fourth ranked in the sporting group. His stud fees now met his handler fees, and a check for an overage arrived sporadically. There was also a single check for her book of ballpark photos, called *Diamonds in the Rough*, which was published in March, during spring training. Locally, it was set out on tables of baseball books that stores displayed when the itch for the rite of spring became acute. And her bitch, Kirby, although not big enough to show for a breed championship, was what the breeder called *birdy*, so she decided to train her for spaniel hunt tests. Together, alone with the dog, out in a brown field of stickers and foxtails, honing the spaniel's natural ability to point, flush and retrieve, she understood the joy of being part of a team, a pleasure she had once rejected. The dog's eyes sparkled in its clownish face, and at home, always bright, found her, whenever she lifted her head, stirred, or involuntarily groaned. The dog slept on the floor on her side of the bed, at her feet under the kitchen table, under the desk she used for the business office, and, in the dark of the darkroom, the dog's fur constantly brushed her leg.

Meanwhile, if her husband's t-shirt or skin or just one hair touched her, she woke immediately. But the book, the dog's field work, and the quickly approaching spring training kept her from dwelling on her marriage night, when she'd tried to let him. She'd thought of herself in the darkroom, pictured herself there, he was just another boy approaching her in the liquid obscurity. Squeezed her eyes shut to manufacture the darkness. But she realized she had her hands braced against his chest, pushing, and gasped, or screamed, she doesn't know which. She pushed harder and twisted, turned herself over, her back to him. She pictured the view of her enlarger and trays, her fingers in developing solution or wielding the black metal dodging/burning tools, and probably would not have flinched. But he cursed once, softly, before jerking himself from the bed and sleeping noisily on the sofa.

But there were other things to pique her attention that year. Another mayor, Rodger Hedgecock—a future popular conservative radio talk host—was indicted for conspiracy. Ray Kroc, venerated McDonald's mastermind and 1974 savior of the doomed Padres, died in January, and his widow wanted to dedicate the season to him. And, as if the corporate angels had decreed, the Padres were winning.

They'd started with a young Tony Gwynn on the cusp of achieving the first of his eight batting titles. Added some tarnished stars from the Yankees and Dodgers—Mr. Clean Steve Garvey cut loose by the Dodgers the year before he set his consecutive game record, and Graig Nettles needing to move on because he authored a Yankee-blasting book called *Balls.* When Goose Gossage likewise abandoned the Yankees and signed with the Padres, someone noted, These days if you don't want to be a Yankee, you have to take a number. There was a shortstop who had once flipped-out and flipped-off his hometown fans now affectionately dubbed "Smooth Operator," the second baseman with a criminal drug record, the slightly-above-average outfielder who'd been chosen before Tony Gwynn in the 1981 amateur draft, miscellaneous others found under the heading *Who Are These Guys?* and a pitching staff that included a card-carrying member of the John Birch Society, a professional bass fisherman, and a left-hander who would in the near future lose his left arm to cancer.

Through the spring and summer—except the week of July 18 when James Huberty killed twenty-one people with a high-power rifle in one of Kroc's crowded San Diego County McDonald's restaurants, at the time the worst mass murder in U.S. history, and caused her and her husband to look at each other for the first time in weeks, with horror—there was usually something vital, something invigorating to float on, or something gratifying to wrestle with: Would Steve Garvey and Graig Nettles be able to shoulder the club's power needs? Would the ten-game suspension of Dick Williams after the multiple on-field mob skirmishes in Atlanta be worth it for the possible incentive, the spark it might provide the August-weary players? Was it possible Terry Kennedy wasn't any better at throwing out base-stealing runners than expansion-draft Fred Kendall and neurotic head-case Mike Ivie of '70s? Which of these current tender personalities needed to be coddled, which needed a boot in the butt? And talk about head cases, would philosopher, physicist, jazz guitarist and neo-Nazi Eric Show keep his on straight for the whole season?

In September, Kirby finished her junior hunter title. Right after that the Padres lost the first two games in Chicago in the League Championship Series. Lost badly. Looked like the Padres of 1970. The newspapers spoke of the end of some kind of century-old curse she'd never heard of. When the team flew back from Chicago and arrived at the stadium on buses at two a.m., she was there with thousands of other people to scream and whoop and whistle and yell and sing "We Are the Champions" and "Let's Get Excited." The sportscasters said the players were overwhelmed by the startling, unanticipated flood of affection and gratitude.

Then she yelped and hugged Kirby for each hit, run scored, and key strikeout during the three home games. When Garvey hit his incredible home run in the ninth inning to win game four, she burst out her front door to shriek toward the sky, and other neighbors had also come outside to shout—just so someone else could hear them—and she could also hear the roar of the sixty thousand people screaming at the stadium. She danced in the street again, waved and shouted from her open car window to strangers on the freeway, after the Padres won a frenzied game five, and had won the pennant.

During 1984, instead of grappling with why her husband never again tried, or agonizing that she was feeling no desire to be touched by anyone other than the dog who licked her mouth whenever she asked for a kiss, she'd only felt listless, or sometimes apprehensive, if Templeton made an error, Gossage blew a lead, or Tony went 0 for 4. In heady 1984 it didn't happen often. And at first, 1985 was more of the same. Especially since the crook who'd almost sent the Padres to Washington finally served his prison sentence. But in July she went to a doctor complaining of chest pains, positive the stabbing sensation was either an imminent heart attack or because the Padres were letting a five-game lead slip away to the Dodgers, and not because her husband had moved out.

It started when Allan Wiggins didn't show up for a game, then missed several games in a row, and they didn't know (or weren't saying) where he was or what had happened, until a reporter broke the story that he was checked into drug rehab. Kroc's philanthropist widow vowed he'd never play for the team again. He was traded before the end of June, just before over sixty canyon-rim houses with views of the stadium in Mission Valley were condensed into piles of ashes in the worst wildfire in city history, a few miles from where she lived. The smoke rising over the treetops looked like a jet crash. On July 13 the Padres were nudged back into second place. On September second it was third place. On September 11, Eric Show, as always petulant, sat in moody insolence on the mound after giving up Pete Rose's record-setting hit in Cincinnati, while the ball was presented to Rose and ovations given. On September 15th the team was in fourth place.

Her male dog, Clay, had never come home. He still won over and over and over. The clumber breeder who'd sold her both dogs said it was time for the bitch to have puppies. But she risked a lawsuit and had the bitch spayed. Because her photography now only brought in half of what it had with her husband helping, she sold the stud dog for a third of a year's dog show photography salary, and 100 times what she made on her book, which had hardly sold any copies. She had one carton of books stored in the darkroom, the rest were remaindered and pulped. She hadn't taken any pictures for a while, except the show stuff she had to do for a living. She threw out the portraits of athletes' faces she'd done in college. It turned out none of them had been Tony Gwynn.

The next two decades went like this:

In 1985, Ed Whitson, who'd opted for free-agency and the hot lights of New York, broke Yankee manager Billy Martin's arm in a bar brawl. In 1989, Dave Dravecky, by then pitching for the Giants, came back as a starter after cancer treatment, but his left arm snapped while throwing a pitch. Ex-socialite Betty Broderick let herself into her ex-husband's apartment and shot him and his new wife and thus became queen of ex-wives across the country—at least for those who had been married for more than a year.

In 1990, Steve Garvey, who'd retired a hero two years before—and the first Padre to have his uniform number retired—had to give up his budding political career and admit to fathering two illegitimate children, in addition to the child carried by his supposed fiancé. All over San Diego, vehicles exhibited bumper stickers proclaiming *Steve Garvey Is Not My Padre!*

In 1991 Clay Kirby died in his hometown. Probably a heart attack. And Allan Wiggins died, possibly of AIDS. Dave Dravecky's cancerous pitching arm was amputated. Eric Show, pitching elsewhere, went on the disabled list for an infected thumb from biting his fingernails.

In 1993, reading elsewhere in the newspaper besides the sports page, she saw a tiny news-blip about a thirty-year-old woman who was suing her high school English teacher for the emotional trauma of a sexual relationship that had occurred when the woman was sixteen. The defendant—the thirty-year-old woman plaintiff's high school English teacher—was the supervising teacher who'd lost interest in his student-teacher in 1979. The thirty-year-old woman would have been sixteen in 1979. When does life begin? he had asked.

Life went on. Except Eric Show died of unknown causes at a drug and alcohol treatment center in 1994.

In 1994, Kirby was diagnosed with breast cancer. Advanced breast cancer in dogs, besides metastasizing, manifests in skin ulcerations. It began with a small patch of what looked like chaffed skin that she treated with antibiotic cream. The ointment attracted Kirby's nose and caused her to lick the area, further irritating it, so Kirby wore boy's underwear, turned backwards to allow her stump tail to come out the fly. Later, on Kirby's underside, from the insides of her thighs up to and including her entire chest, belly and loin, the formerly soft white epidermis was a combination of hard red lumps, and dry cracked-open lesions oozing clear fluid.

With Kirby on her back, towels tucked all around, she washed Kirby's groin with antibiotic shampoo. She used a soft mitt originally intended for polishing silver trophies. Rinsed with warm water. Patted dry with a linen dish towel. Sometimes blood seeped slowly from either an invisible perforation or from one of the lesions. She used various combinations of calamine lotion, medicated powder, Bactine, rubbing alcohol, hydrogen peroxide, and something called Liquid Bandage that smelled like varnish. The calamine lotion was to protect the ulcerated skin and block potential seepage. The powders to soothe and absorb. The Bactine to anesthetize. The alcohol and hydrogen peroxide as cleaning agents to remove the previous day's treatment. Beyond the ulcerations, the dog's hocks were puffy, swollen with fluid, so she massaged Kirby's legs and could feel, between her palms, the fragile bones of Kirby's feet and ankles begin to emerge from the swelling. She watched and stroked Kirby's face throughout the procedure—checking for signs of pain. While waiting for the calamine to dry, she grazed Kirby's chest with her fingertips and caressed the insides of her ears.

Meanwhile, for more than a decade, it was the heart of Tony's career. Stealing five bases in a single game, and setting a Major League record when he and two other Padres lead off a game with back-to-back-to-back home runs. Going 3-for-4 and 4-for-5, not just once but over and over, then his second league-leading batting average at .370. Breaking-up no hitters in the eighth or ninth. Another year, another batting title secured with a 3-for-4 on the last day of the season to beat the man he was tied with—who'd sat out the game, hoping Tony would be oh-for. Five hits in a game for the fourth time in one season. Batting .394 and on a tear, a .400 batting title eminent, when the players union called a strike in 1994. When the season ended early, and the playoffs and World Series were cancelled, experts said fans would have to forgive the players, would have to be won over, would have to be seduced all over again. She'd been an easy conquest.

Tony came back in 1995 for another batting title, and another one in 1996—when the Republicans finally gave the city its National Convention, and the symphony went bankrupt—and his eighth batting title in 1997, including his career's ninth game with five or more hits, third on the all-time list. Two years later his 3,000th hit.

But before that, in 1998, after scoring decisive victories in the first three games of the League Championship Series against the Atlanta Braves, the Padres lost the fourth game but had a lead in the seventh inning of the fifth game. Sitting still in a chair was out of the question. Likewise incapable of standing in one place, she paced a circle through her house muttering *please, please, please, please* which shifted to *no, no, no, no* . . . A few walks, a few well-placed hits, the lead disappeared and she flung herself onto her bed, overcome with strange sobbing. After her anticlimax divorce, there was no risk she would ever marry again; she didn't have to make an oath. After holding her dog's face close to hers while a vet injected the animal with a fatal dose of barbiturates, she did not tacitly profess that she could not allow herself to form another attachment with a pet that would only lead to this desolate grief over its loss. But on her bed in 1988 she vowed she could not afford to love a baseball team again.

The Padres did eventually win the National League Pennant in the sixth game against the Braves. Boomeranged back to euphoria, but in the World Series they were swept in four games by the Yankees, losing a game-one lead, then losing heart. All except Tony. He was eight for fifteen.

Two decades after she took sports photos while he played basketball, she got to meet Tony Gwynn, at a book signing. His book signing, not hers. She waited in line for over two hours. He was only scheduled to sign books for an hour and a half. At the time he was supposed to leave, Tony came out, surveyed the line of people extending outside the bookstore and curled around the food court, called out "Okay, let's do it!" and returned to his table to sign every book, baseball card and ball. Then it was her turn, and she had a fleeting moment to say something to him. She sputtered, "Thank you for staying in San Diego." He handed her an autographed book, smiled and said "Thank *you*."

She started taking photos again. Bought a season ticket and arrived early at the ballpark to take self portraits: in a row of empty seats in the outfield with the green of center field over her shoulder, spooning relish at the same messy hotdog condiment stand, standing at the top end of an aisle in the upper deck, gazing out from the huge circular concrete ramps where fans drained out after a game; or just her arm and hand, with a Brooks Robinson mitt, extended beyond the rail to catch a pop foul.

1985

The wreckage of the Titanic was located and a hole in the ozone was discovered. Rock Hudson died of AIDS and missing children decorated milk cartons.

What If

The neighborhood was on fire.

The neighborhood was called Normal Heights. It had once been the location of the old normal school, and it sat on a plateau above the county's major river valley, thus normal-plus-heights. No one thought the neighborhood's name was odd, although few, if anyone, knew that normal schools had been started by the French in the seventeenth century, and the English adjective "normal" derived from the Latin word *normal*, which signifies a carpenter's square, a rule, a pattern or model. Teacher-training schools were called *normal* because they were to be *model* schools in which pupils apply theory to practice. Puritans, starting colleges in America, wanted only *practical* education, nothing too ethereal, abstract, speculative, and . . . useless.

So it was an old neighborhood, as old goes in Southern California. The streets were lined with palm trees and eucalyptus, jacaranda and Brazilian pepper. The one business district along Adams Avenue had pizza and Chinese take-out, Mexican hole-in-the-wall cafes that would've been called *cantinas* if they were in Mazatlan, a vegetarian restaurant run by a suspect group of possibly brainwashed young men, and a produce-plus-health-food corner grocery. There had been a Polish restaurant once, but such places, offering large sausages, hadn't survived in California in the '70s. Just off Adams Avenue, about three blocks on a residential street, a small walled monastery overlooked the valley.

You could walk to the post office and pass antique shops, used bookstores, and three laundromats where the thick steamy smell of clean cotton wafted out the doors and young women just like you stood over heaps of miniature sets of pants, overalls and t-shirts, their bangs plastered to their foreheads. There was a bar called *Elbow Inn*. And another one called *Paddy's Wagon*. There was a spiritual healer who read palms and tarot cards and offered midwifery, and a pet store called *The Blue Lagoon*. There were courtyards where five or six identical, miniature Spanish-style cottages were arranged around a square of grass, one with a fountain that no longer ran now used as a planter for geraniums. There was a closet-sized establishment that sold only juices of any combination: celery-and-carrot, mango-and-lettuce, tomato-lime.

If you walked the other way, you'd go by a real estate and law office—small storefronts, with brick planters of marigolds and petunias beside their doors. Then a few thrift stores, a copy shop with only two Xerox machines behind a counter, a model train store, and—across the bridge that spanned the freeway—a library, a community vegetable garden, and a bookstore that had been the first in the country to have a coffee shop inside, featuring a large selection of gay magazines not carried by the library. Beside the bookstore, a one-screen theatre where you had seen *A Hard Day's Night* as a first-run movie when you were eight, and now could probably see it again since the theatre showed classic and cult movies, a different pair every night, and published a calendar that everyone in the neighborhood had stuck to their refrigerator with a magnet.

Where you'd grown up, the place you'd left when you left home, not too many years before this, there were no sidewalks or juice stores or natural groceries or landmark theaters. People had chickens and big rocky, weedy hillside yards where they could fabricate a shelter and a barbed wire fence and have a horse. For ten or twenty years after leaving home, there's little nostalgia about where you came from; you get caught up with the striking-out-on-your-own, the discovering who you are and what you have to offer and who's going to want it, and you don't do too much longing for what you left behind. So it didn't matter a lot that nobody in Normal Heights had a horse. Instead, there were a lot of cats, sitting in windows of living rooms and storefronts, on stoops, on fences, and sometimes dead. Once someone's cat had gone up a fifty-foot palm tree. Not one of those smooth slender palm trees that bend over in hurricanes, but the kind with a thick jagged façade caused by cutting off the dead lower fronds as the tree grew higher, so the trunk was like a huge cylindrical cheese grater until the skirt of leaves at the top where the cat's face looked down. It could've been your cat, if you had a cat, and after trying to lure it down with a can of sardines extended on a tree-trimming device a neighbor donated, something else had to be done. Fire trucks no longer came for treed cats. In a neighborhood with nothing taller than two stories, fire trucks didn't have ladders, did they? But somehow someone got the idea to call an antenna repairman, and he went up with boots and leather gloves, ropes and a pulley, climbing the way he would scale a sheer rock face, got the cat into a canvas bag and lowered it to the ground. That cat lived, for a while longer. But while walking to the post office or laundromat or juice store, you would often see one in the gutter, sometimes just skin and hair, other times swollen and staring, a frozen snarl aimed skyward, the buzzing of amassed flies like a wind-up motor still sputtering inside it. But probably most of the time someone found the cat still fresh and carried it home. One time a woman screamed and screamed in the street for several hours after a cat was mauled by a pizza delivery car. No one could even tell if the cat was hers, because someone else wrapped the body in a towel and held it while the screaming woman went on screaming. It was a day that didn't sound like Normal Heights and people came out of houses and apartments to ask her to shut up. Meanwhile the pizza delivery boy sat on the curb beside the woman with the dead cat wrapped in a towel until his pizzas were cold.

A funky Normal Heights version of Monopoly might've seemed fun at first, with the spiritual advisor and massage therapist as the cheap-rent Baltic and Mediterranean Avenues, and the theatre with carved gilded woodwork and velvet-draped balcony seats as the Boardwalk. But it would've been all wrong. First of all, across the bridge, the theater and gay bookstore and library did not like to be called Normal Heights; they said they were in *Kensington.* If you lived in Normal Heights you probably couldn't afford to live in Kensington, although you could use their library, view their classic movies, and sip the coffee in their bookstore. Maybe that part was like Monopoly, but it wasn't like Normal Heights. A Normal Heights Monopoly game would have to have a different way to win: no one who lived in Normal Heights was striving to own all of Normal Heights and raise the rents so high that no one else could afford to live there, then squeeze the money out of everyone until they all had to move away. Maybe somebody wanted to live there forever.

You would love living in Normal Heights, even if it could not be forever. Even if nothing happened to change the course of your life, the rhythm of the journey you'd already started probably would've taken you to another neighborhood someday, by the time you turned thirty, a neighborhood that was different but good, or even better, in its own way. A neighborhood that could've saved your marriage.

From the neighborhood down to the valley, the walls of the canyon were native semi-arid chaparral, home to possums and snakes, birds and coyote, some foxes, feral cats who'd survived the streets of Normal Heights and now would be food for the coyote, and one mythical albino deer, but it hadn't been seen for years until it was spotted once again farther west toward Presidio Park, where it was hit by a car. The floor of the valley used to be dairy farms beside a creek they called a river. Photos from a hundred years ago showed the entire valley filled with water when the sluggish stream proved its ultimate authority. Even Southern California has its hundred-year floods. Now the valley had a freeway and hotels, two shopping malls, a small convention center, a tiny golf course whose days were numbered because the land was too valuable for pitch-n-putt, and a stadium.

In the stadium that day there would be a baseball game, and after the game, a concert performed by the symphony. Naturally you'd be going to both events in the stadium, because your husband played a brass instrument in the symphony. Brass instruments are expensive, but nothing like violins and cellos, which can cost as much as a house, even houses in California, if the instrument is good enough. So the string players, playing an outdoor concert, always used their second rate instruments—called, affectionately, their *axes*. Brass players frequently only had one ax. Of course his ax would be in the car when you headed off to the stadium on the day Normal Heights was on fire.

It was what he did, play a horn in a symphony, and probably would be what he got to do forever. You know he had to be good to play in a symphony, to be allowed to do for a living the thing he felt best doing. With roughly thirty symphonies in the country that paid a living wage—and in this case it meant a salary that allowed him to live in Normal Heights but not La Jolla, La Mesa, La Costa, or even down the street in Kensington— and hundreds if not thousands of musicians vying for each seat in each orchestra, he had to be good. He was lucky, that way. Fortunate, blessed, privileged. Even though you knew he'd worked for it.

Remember: you had made a game, a board game, based on the practical life of a classical musician. Each player tried to get into bigger and bigger orchestras, starting with community orchestras, then regional, on up to small cities, etcetera. For each audition at each level, the player had to have gathered enough poker chips representing lessons (paid for with money earned at freelance gigs) and hours practicing (earned by landing on the proper squares on the board or gaining practice hours via the "phone-call" and "mail" stacks of cards). The auditions were based on roll of the dice, with wider and wider odds as the size of the orchestra increased. It was an elaborate, multi-faceted game that could go all night and on into the next, when you would play it with other friends from the symphony, each time tweaking the rules a little to smooth out the rough spots. No player ever won the game by obtaining a chair in one of the top six or-chestras, but still, they had jobs in this city's real orchestra, which was more than hundreds of musicians in this city and thousands of others all over the country could say.

But it wouldn't be fair if he was the only one accomplishing what he set out to do. That particular summer, that particular day, it could've been a week or even just a day before you would hit that *finally-finally-finally* phase of euphoria, when, in the nick of time, just before you turned thirty, you'd get the call: your first one-woman show or exhibit or book. It might've been sculpted ceramics—mostly abstract figures of wild horses with legs and necks too long, too thin, or too thick, and manes like plumes of smoke. Or maybe it was multi-colored leather marti-gras masks, cut, formed, fringed, dyed, hardened into shape, grinning, sneering, frowning, aghast, horrified, leering. Or poems. Poems about horses and angst, tem-pests and sex, sex and earthquakes, ennui and sex, lust and horses, stallions and flowers, petals and stamen, pistil and pollination. *Finally-finally-finally*, the garden you'd tilled since the scent of its verdant soil first caressed your nostrils in college would *have* to bear fruit, pay in the breakthrough div-idends of continued flowering-to-fruit-bearing metaphors. It had to be-cause . . . *you'd* also put in the hours and had taken the lessons. And when it happened, someday, the most important dividend would be that no longer would you be spending any chilly hours answering phones and directing calls to auto salesmen and mechanics at the Ford dealership on El Cajon Boulevard that really couldn't claim to be part of Normal Heights. You'd walk away singing the jingle for the final time—See *Pearson Ford, We Stand Alone at Fairmount and El Cajon*—and the next house, in Mis-sion Hills or Hillcrest or even Kensington, might have a full extra bed-room, maybe two, and a second bathroom, and a two-car garage that could become an even more invigorating workshop; you'd no longer be walking to the post office or laundromat, and there'd be no smaller house in the backyard sheltering another musician waiting for his turn to earn a living wage in a symphony. It shouldn't have been the fire—nor the house in the backyard, nor the less-successful musician in that house in the back-yard—but success that impelled you away from Normal Heights.

It started long before the baseball game, on the side of the long, mean-dering road called *Camino del Rio South* that ran almost the length of the valley, just slightly up the rise of the southern canyon wall. The freeway in the river bottom was north of and also lower than Camino del Rio, and the former pastures and shopping centers and golf course and stadium were north of the freeway, then the river itself on the far northern side of the valley, was at least two, maybe four miles away from the road named road-of-the-river. Offices and restaurants and hotels had collected along Camino del Rio, but sometimes, between parking lots, the wild hillside still extended all the way from Normal Heights at the top to the sidewalk that snaked beside Camino del Rio where the maids who cleaned the hotel rooms, and the gardeners and cooks and janitors walked from the bus stops to work.

A cigarette thrown from a passing car. It was during a July Santa Ana wind, blowing in off the desert. July could easily be hot, but usually it was September when you felt the wind named for the Santa Ana Canyon, itself named by the settlers of Santa Ana California after Saint Anne, not Antonio Lopez de Santa Ana Perez de Lebron, the opium addict who'd defeated the Texans at the Alamo. Canyons like the Santa Ana help chan-nel the hot dry desert winds toward the coast, thus accelerated their speed. But Santa Ana wasn't the only canyon. The big wide river valley with the freeway and the stadium, called Mission Valley, was a canyon, a shallow, smooth canyon, but on its eastern end it connected to the more severe Mission Gorge, and Mission Gorge was the real canyon that conveyed the winds that dried the grasses and brush on the side of the roads, like Camino del Rio South, where a cigarette was thrown from a passing car.

The wild oats—having shed their seeds and dried to paper husks—the sage and brown tumbleweeds, the sumac and Father Serra's mustard crackled briefly in flame then crumbled to ashes as the snaky line of flame edged up the wall of the valley. Up there, in Normal Heights, the num-bered streets, 30th, 31st, 32nd, 33rd, 34th, 35th, 36th, and the named streets in between, were all flat on a level plane, and they crossed the east-west business district of Adams Avenue then ended in cul-de-sacs north of the thrift shops and laundromats and natural grocery, above the south rim of Mission Valley. Those fortunate few houses on the cul-de-sacs had yards that extended into the canyon, mostly left to the indigenous flora to flourish right up to the border landscape bushes surrounding their lawns, and the masses of eucalyptus that made their shade.

The eucalyptus trees were brought to Southern California to grow as a crop for railroad ties, but the wood proved too soft for that purpose. So the trees grew tall and thick on the property lines of ranchos, and the former crop groves became shady parks. The trees thrived in the dry climate, and were a way to turn Southern California green, leafy and forested. Planted everywhere, a new sapling in every new yard, they quickly grew huge, and those in Normal Heights were easily thirty or forty years old or more. They're drought-resistant because their tough leaves are full of oil instead of water. In the Santa Ana winds they flutter like aspens, and rattle like bones. The lick of one flame, and—*boom*—the tree is a blazing oil-soaked torch. As the brush fire rippled up the side of Mission Valley . . . *boom . . . boom, boom . . . boom* . . . the eucalyptus trees making shady yards at the ends of the cul-de-sacs in Normal Heights exploded.

Not only did the fire trucks in Normal Heights have no ladders, the fire hydrants in Normal Heights had little or no water pressure. This could have been because the original lots were deep, and the houses small. During the postwar boom years, a lot of people built another, smaller house at the back of their property (thus the abode in your backyard). Then parents of the '40s and '50s who'd raised their families in Normal Heights died or moved to retirement homes, and the houses had become too small for contemporary families, the neighborhood too multihued— the same people who would be mowing their lawns in La Jolla might live next door in Normal Heights. And who wanted to raise a family with a musician living in the little house in the back yard? But someone would still buy the lot and either rent the house, or both houses; or sometimes remove the house, or both houses, and build a low-rise apartment. The same amount of water that used to fill and re-fill one toilet, or two, now filled twelve or eighteen.

Water conservation was constant, as were the reminders. Use a car wash that recycles its water . . . don't sweep with a hose . . . water lawns at dusk or overnight, every other day at most . . . *If it's yellow, let it mellow* . . . But still, the number of residents had easily quintupled since the grid of streets and sewer lines and water pipes and single-family homes had first been sketched on blue tissue paper. Firemen jumped from trucks and attached hoses to hydrants only to be met with a thin trickle oozing from the nozzle they aimed at the next fully engulfed house.

It was still before the baseball game. If you stood in your front yard, ash and cinders blew past, hitting you like fleeing insects. A wall of smoke rose from the northern side of Normal Heights. Helicopters dove, zig-zagged and hovered. Tanker airplanes droned. The radio had news every half hour, and every broadcast began with the fire. Twelve houses gone, then twenty, then twenty-three. Threatening to advance south, leap over Adams Avenue, and continue to incinerate the numbered streets, hopping from the dry top of one palm tree to the next, from one brittle shake roof to the next, from one incendiary eucalyptus to the next.

But it was time to go, if you were going to the baseball game before the concert. The concert was not optional, it was his opportune job, but attending the baseball game was not mandatory. If you lived south of Adams Avenue, especially between Adams and Madison, what were the chances, really, of the fire cremating everything between the gorge and Madison Street, including everything inside that little house in the middle of the block on 36th street with another smaller quarters housing another musician in the backyard. And if you stayed, what could you do, really, to stop it? On the radio, they were begging residents to not turn on their hoses, stop flushing toilets, resist taking a cooling shower, don't wash your clothes or cars or dogs today, not today!

There was a box game you'd had for a while, a municipal management game, where each player ran a small city and had to make decisions about things like how much police and fire protection to maintain, water supplies and landfill capacity, sewer water treatment and recycling—or choose to pipe it elsewhere; determine regulations for factory and car emissions, for suburban development, for curbside trash hauling, or just wait for the wind to blow your smog to the next player's town. It had been almost impossible to understand the game, then to win it, and you might've thought of revamping it, if you hadn't realized it was geared that way on purpose: any player who tried to prioritize ecology would lose. But still, if you'd kept the game, you might've learned enough, over the years, through the water shortages and recycling programs and fires, to fix it.

That was the kind of game you liked best, though. Not two-person-only games, but games combining both skill and chance, where you had to make decisions and also deal with sudden information, good or bad. Games with complication, even drama. What role could you play in checkers? Sometimes, on concert nights, the musician-in-the-backyard who hadn't been good and lucky enough to earn a living wage in the symphony, came over to play games. But with just the two of you, it was hard to make even the box games—Fortune 400 and The Bottom Line and that city management game—rousing enough, and Trivial Pursuit was okay, if you had enough grass, but that was usually for after concerts, at someone else's house, with the rest of the lucky earning-a-living-wage musicians. The ones who were playing the concert after the baseball game at the stadium the day of the fire.

What else could you do, that day, but lock your house as usual, and, through the back door notice the long eye-shaped crack in the backyard musician's blinds as he jealously watched your husband go to another concert for which he was paid a living wage, even though the paid musicians grumbled and moaned about having to play classical "pops," the uncomplicated stuff, in difficult places like a stadium where the string players had to use their second-best ax because the cheesy fireworks they had to include to make that kind of audience think they enjoyed a symphony concert might char their best ax.

The cars filed into the stadium in the valley as usual. Your seats, as usual, the cheap ones in the upper deck. (A living wage for doing the thing he loved was one thing, box seats quite another.) You wouldn't usually sit in the very top row of the upper deck, but today was different. From up there, from above the right field corner, if you stood and faced away from the playing field—out over the concrete wall behind the last seats, past the parking lot and the blur of freeway and the hazy low office buildings along Camino del Rio South, up the side of the hill to the crest—you could count the number of black smudges that used to be houses, and you could see those still burning, dozens of them, a skyline of flame where once the skyline of roofs had been enshrouded in dense shrubs and trees. Over seventy of them in all. Only the monastery had a wall, not previously visible through the brush on the outside. Only the monastery was not burning.

Was anyone who lived on the rim of the canyon in Normal Heights at the baseball game that day? And if so, if it were you, would you stay to hear the symphony play its summer classics: "William Tell," "Bolero," "Stars and Stripes Forever," and "The 1812 Overture"? Would you cringe at each pop and blast of fireworks in the newly darkened sky? Was the hillside still glowing in the distance? When you returned home, would you be astonished, or was it only the inevitable you came back to see?

Adams Avenue was gloomy with hanging smoke, with dirty water in the gutters, with closed shops and ashy sidewalks. No one would blame you for not looking to see if any cats had crawled to the curb today to die. You might have more selfish concerns, and anyway, no one was screaming. Not anymore. After everything is gone, you tend to just stand and stare, poke at sooty debris with one foot, smash the blind eye of the skeletal TV with a black brick.

Okay, forget renters insurance, which you would've never had. Forget about the Salvation Army and friends coming to the rescue with clothes and bedding. Forget about The Red Cross and group-camping in a high school auditorium and free government surplus food (those huge bricks of orange cheese). When everything is gone, it's *gone*.

Gone: the leather masks, the ceramic abstract equines with contorted bodies waiting to be transported to the gallery (the fire too hot, they would be black, blistered, cracked, and even more contorted, if not complete rubble). Gone: the poems about hothouse orchids and heavy-breathing stallions, mosaics made of the parts from old manual typewriters and rotary telephones, the play about a musician who lives in the backyard of another musician, or the long hand-dyed cotton skirts with strings of prancing ponies hand-stitched around the hem.

So what if you still had your job at Pearson Ford. It was only a job to work at while you waited for the other stuff to lift you out. You were supposed to quit, when you started to live off the fruits of your passion, at least by the time you turned thirty. But if the passion had burned up, had helped fuel the searing fire, had in fact made the fire more intense, had kept the blaze crackling as long as possible, maybe even longer than it would've burned otherwise, it (the zeal) was now not buried and waiting to be found in the residue of your former sneakers and leather hiking boots, in the black debris of your former crock-pot and electric wok you'd gotten as wedding gifts, in the ashes of your former bricks-n-boards and the books that sat on the shelves they made, in the stink of the black mud that used to be your second-hand sofa. *It* was not just damaged . . . it was gone.

Now what do you do? You think this is some kind of game? And when it's over, when you lose or figure out the game can't be won, you just go back to Normal Heights and walk to the grocery store for wheat germ bread, buy a carrot juice, then some stamps, pick up a lost kitten crying in the shrubs outside the laundromat and feed it Tender Vittles and give it a flea bath and let your husband name it *You-Little-Nudnik*?

No, now is the time to be practical. For solutions. For survival.

Remember, going to college in the late '70s, do you recall any career advisors? If they existed, they were the loneliest desk-squatters in the university, because no one was thinking about careers, not in that way. It was do-what-you're-good-at, do-what-fulfills-you, do-what-makes-you-like-yourself. For some it was music, and that was a career, and could, for the lucky ones, pay a living wage, (or if they failed, they would have to live in smaller houses behind the small houses in Normal Heights and give music lessons in the back rooms of piano stores). For the others it was sociology, theatre, recreation, dance, art, literature, design, or liberal arts. No, there weren't any underwater basket weaving classes—a popular yuppie myth when the next generation came to school in these Reagan-'80s and deluged then saturated the business colleges and pre-law. By the time these Reaganites arrived on campus, you and your husband were out, *doing* it, living in Normal Heights.

Who said only the musicians could go out and *do* the indulgent thing you studied in college? So you get a job to help make money for rent and food, and keep doing the real thing in your *spare* time, which was your *real* time. And your husband the musician—one of those fortunate ones—even though they'd made him take ROTC in that conformist Southern state college he'd gone to before coming west for graduate school where you met him, he would never have to fall back on that or anything else. He had his living wage from the symphony, enough to rent a one-and-a-half bedroom house on 36th street in Normal Heights that came with another one-bedroom cottage in the backyard on the alley housing another musician—but this one not doing as well in the Practical-Life-of-a-Musician game, no living wage, just the lessons he gave in a piano store. And that extra half bedroom in your street-facing house—a perfect studio, for you, wasn't it? It was where those poems or those masks or those flamboyant ceramic horses had been shaped. (Maybe the detached shed that used to be a one-car garage would be better for the masks and ceramics. The washer and dryer that no longer worked were a perfect workbench, despite the grooves in the metal made by the lids, but there was a utility sink with running water, and electricity. It could've also been a darkroom, a hothouse, a woodworking shop, or a drafting room for the design of board games. It could've also been another shack to house another musician.)

So you came-of-age after the draft ended, lived the you-can-do-any-thing life of a middle-class baby-boomer for twenty years, then it was a day job and living paycheck-to-paycheck without mom-and-dad's subsidy in the proletarian-meets-bohemian enclave of Normal Heights. But *survival?*

Before Normal Heights and the former normal school university, in more childish days in the bedroom you were loaned in your parents' house, you'd once thought, with some puerile comfort, that if you found no one to marry you, and if you were unable to find work traveling with the Lipizzaner stallions or tending botanic gardens at the zoo, there was always the military as a safety net. (You had this thought even though your more up-to-the-minute used-to-be-a-normal-school state university in California wouldn't dare force anyone to join ROTC. Even your husband's out-of-touch Southern state college that mandated ROTC didn't require it for *girls*.) But if you found yourself unemployed and unattached, this was a military town and there it was: It could give you a job and pay you. But that was between Vietnam and the Gulf War, years of some modicum of peace—if you didn't count Africa and the Middle East and Afghanistan—and it didn't sound *too* bad, as long as you didn't say it out loud or admit it to anyone. The ads on TV had made it look sublime. Like you could maneuver the signal flags as jets came in at sunset to land on carriers in silent slow motion. You could be a nurse in scrub suit and surgical mask side-by-side with a doctor under glaring lights—no uniform, no *yessir, nosir* when the doctor asked for the next instrument, only his respectful eyes appreciating your skill. (How was it obvious the ad wasn't offering the doctor's job as a military option?) You could even twirl a white rifle—it wouldn't be a *real* rifle—in a parade, or be a pastry chef, or play in a band or orchestra. They made it sound like you wouldn't be crawling under barbed wire in the mud, and certainly like you wouldn't find yourself in South Korea or Libya. By 1985, though, you'd be almost thirty. Your secret military backup ship had sailed.

If you were going to be sensible, your first thought might have been teaching. But no, not that. Not because those who can't *do*, teach; but because those who teach don't *do*. Don't have time to, if they're worth a damn. Even if the fire meant you would no longer *do*, you wanted to have *time* to do, if you ever decided to do again. But still, you could've considered substitute teaching or parochial schools, or substitute teaching at parochial schools; maybe the monastery had a school tied to it? After all, you had gone to the university that had grown out of the old normal school. But had taken nothing practical, except maybe the letter-press printing class in the graphic arts department, even though offset was long established as the industry norm.

There probably aren't any letter press printers looking for help from burned-out poetic orchid-growing stallion-sculptors who took one letterpress class as an elective (you still had the business cards you'd made for yourself there). What are the other things you thought about?

Real horses. You never got to have one. Really, so few kids ever got that pony that's supposed to guarantee childhood is sweet. Wished for one every Christmas, but you always knew a shaggy little Shetland wouldn't show up in a paddock built overnight in your dad's backyard. Someone up the street had a mule her parents rented for six months. To be a jockey now, you would've had to earn your way in as an exercise rider. (Never mind that there hadn't at this point been any female jockeys yet, there had probably been female exercise riders). To be an exercise rider you would probably have to earn your way in as a stable hand. And plodding up the street on that girl's mule one or twice, or going to see the Lipizzaner stallions when you were six, or writing a few flabby poems about arching necks and flaring nostrils, then standing at the rail once or twice a year at the Del Mar track eating cheese puffs and yelling *go-go-go* didn't count.

Okay: then, cats. *You-Little-Nudnik* had been contentedly leaving his hair on any horizontal surface and his claw marks on any vertical one, when he might've ended up coyote-chow or a grease spot in the gutter. That's because of you. So your good deed could be expanded into a cat-rescue organization. Lost or abandoned or born wild: lure them in with Tender Vittles, de-flea them and introduce them to a litter box, then out the door to happy homes or adoptive businesses who might cover your cost of food and flea-foam, or the occasional vet bill when you find one who can't defend himself in a screech-and-slash because his last owner had his claws removed. Plus collect donations from the community, from the shops along Adams Avenue who would be grateful for your twice daily road kill patrols, who knew a live cat in a storefront window might bring in customers, but a dead one in the gutter was nothing but repulsion (especially if someone couldn't stop screaming). And you could do it all from home, from the half-bedroom-converted-into-a-studio converted again into an office.

But wait. You're only doing this because of the fire—the fire that burned over seventy houses in Normal Heights one June day in 1985, and if yours was among them, there'd be no back half bedroom from which to run your grass-roots cat-rescue operation. Same goes for the orchid hothouse, or the craft shop making detailed miniature leather saddles for plastic horse statues that little girls get for Christmas instead of real ponies, or the come-watch-TV-with-me service for lonely-hearts in the evenings while your musician husband is playing a concert and other musicians who don't make a living wage are not.

So take a look for a minute at the musician in the hut in the backyard, and what would *he* do if it had all incinerated. He was already balding in his twenties, on the portly side, pear-shaped with a large reddish nose. He just couldn't draw a winning card. And even though nothing of any real value would have burned, when he looked for a new place to live, it couldn't be an apartment, *had* to be a little shack-like house—like the one with termite weakened frame and paint-peeling siding that would have made no more than a black smudge in the ashy lawn of your backyard— because he practiced that brass instrument hours a day (collecting practice hours in the Practical-Life-of-a-Musician game so he could go to auditions and try to earn a living wage someday) and neighbors in apartments tended to complain about the noise. In fact, neighbors in neighborhoods with cracker box houses built before World War II also tended to complain, but if your closest neighbor was the brass-playing earning-a-living-wage musician in the house in front of yours, who would say anything? *That's* what had been razed for the musician in the backyard, because he couldn't move with you and your husband and Nudnik the rescued cat when you found yourself a living-room-kitchen-bedroom converted chicken coop in someone else's backyard elsewhere on the fringes of Normal Heights. Or maybe outside those fringes. Way over close to El Cajon Boulevard, in the nebulous sprawl of other neighborhoods with less evocative personality, but you could still walk to the post office on Adams Avenue where you would keep a PO box with a Normal Heights zip code. And where you could walk to work singing *At Pearson Ford, we stand alone, at Fairrrr-mount and El Cajon.*

OK you're back here again. Games go round-and-round in circles (or squares). And if that's what you're going to do, maybe that's where you should look. *That's* the solution. What if you put the life-of-a-musician game into the car before you went to the baseball game? What if you were going to take it to someone's house after the concert after the baseball game? Maybe the Practical-Life-of-a-Musician game had undergone some recent tweaking and needed another play-through to check the pacing. Maybe the musician from the house in the backyard would even be there. Maybe you needed the opinion of one of those who never did get to earn a living wage playing concerts, even tacky concerts after baseball games, and instead had to force-feed music lessons to bratty monsters in the back room of a piano-and-organ store. Of course the test run-through of the game (not the baseball game) would be called off—that poor musician-in-the-backyard was never going to learn this game. But when you finished kicking the black bricks and trying to dust the soot from your palms onto the sooty thighs of your jeans; when you finished staring at the blob of black goo that used to be your record albums and was still a little warm and malleable—perhaps it could've been shaped into a thoroughbred's arrogant head or the thrashing figure of a stallion, but you didn't touch it—when you finished digging cinders out of your eyes looking for a tear, you would realize what's important: that in the car you still had: Your husband's ax. And the game.

You saved the game. The game isn't gone. You could set up a game-maker studio and go on improving it, developing it. Devote all your time to it. And now, this whole experience makes you realize what you had devised before is only the basis for a bigger game: The Living-a-Practical-Life-in-Normal-Heights Game. A little bit of Monopoly, a little bit of that impossible-to-win city-planning game, and not just the practical lives of musicians but of all who subsist in Normal Heights.

Like Monopoly, there will be properties, but of course, you'll be renting, not buying. There won't be any railroads or utility companies available. Buying residential property could be the eventual goal, except that as soon as someone owns real estate in Normal Heights, they usually leave Normal Heights then rent their property to someone else (you), or knock down a house and build a set of eight apartments, or add a cottage to the backyard and collect two rents. All that could come later, if the game gets that far. Suffice it to say, how you make your money to pay your rent is not from collecting rents from other players, even if you have a musician living in a shack in your backyard.

But you'll have to decide where your money is coming from. This means—how would they say it at the career counseling center at the normal-school-turned-university?—your livelihood, your profession, your vocation, your calling, your way of being yourself. The Practical-Life-in-Normal-Heights Game lets you choose from a whole plethora of pursuits besides classical musician: from the janitors, maids, cooks, and busboys in the offices, hotels and restaurants on Camino del Rio South, just down the canyon wall from Normal Heights . . . to the antenna repairman, pizza delivery driver, the midwife palm-reader, the possibly brain-washed young men who run the vegetarian restaurant. You could mow the lawns in the courtyards of the Spanish-style cottages, or be one of the girls who make the juice assortments, a bartender at *Elbow Inn*, a monk at the monastery . . . or live the practical life of an artiste who paints unicorns on black velvet and sells them on weekends at the gas station on the corner diagonally across from Pearson Ford (singing, *we stand alone, at Fairrr-mount and El Cajon*).

But, at least at first, you can't choose to be anyone who *owns* the juice store or natural grocery, nor an antique shop, and you can't choose to be any of the real estate agents, or lawyers, or the gay bookstore owner . . . they probably don't live in Normal Heights. People who don't live there shouldn't be making all the decisions. That's why you're adding the city-planning aspect to this game. Not a mayor and city council—Normal Heights is a neighborhood, not a self-sufficient city—but just some practical decisions. When the neighborhood meeting card is picked, you have to all get together to determine things like: how much you'll each kick in for how many police officers and firefighters? How much will everyone have to pay for electricity and water and garbage removal? (The musician in the house in the backyard liked to say that maybe there's no need for sanctioned trash removal because Vietnamese refugees go up and down the alley, scavenging from the useless things people pile out there—it's how you got rid of that already-second-hand green sofa where you and the musician-in-the-backyard got bored playing Trivial Pursuit.) The game will have to have a mechanism to make these decisions have an impact on other aspects of the practical life of the player, even though you never really got to decide how many firehouses to maintain in Normal Heights, or the density of residential development in ratio to the decades-old sewer and water and streets-and-sanitation infrastructure. The first and obvious impact of these decisions is less money at each player's payday, but also maybe you'll have to miss your turn, miss one out of every five turns, if water is rationed or if you decide to go with Neighborhood Watch and volunteer paramedics and firehouse.

Meanwhile, for whatever occupation you choose, on your turn you go about the board collecting the things you'll need to do better at it . . . and collecting more things to do even better . . . like the practice hours and auditions for musicians. It would be broken-antenna customers (who might also need their cats rescued from palm trees), or brainwashed vegetarian converts, or newly-invented juice combinations, or successful at-home natural births (the unsuccessful ones are going to cost you), or horse-loving art-buyers. You're trying to land on the important squares that provide these rewards, and avoid the annoying *phone call* and *mail* squares, where you have to draw a card and do what it says, even though sometimes the phone will bring a musician an extra freelance gig, providing money for another lesson; or the mail might bring an acceptance from an art magazine that's using your sixth grade rendition of a kicking steed on its cover.

And then, maybe someday, when you're doing real well—one of those blessed scant minority who win an audition and are paid a living wage, or you're exhibited or published or promoted to housekeeping-supervisor or head-brainwashed-waiter, or recruited to run the orchid hothouse at the zoo—instead of moving out of Normal Heights, you'll be buying property and staying (this is one objective of the game) and it's always better if *you* own the house with another house in the backyard with an unsuccessful musician living in it. Unless you make the mistake of sleeping with him because you feel sorry for him—that'll be a card some hapless street-facing resident will draw, because it could wreak havoc, unless, first, the fire card is drawn.

Yes, at some point during the game—you don't know when, and you don't know who—someone will draw the fire card. And then . . . Literalists may want to actually strike a match and the game will easily burn. See who saves what. See what's imperative to whom. It's a one-of-a-kind game, maybe the best thing you ever made, but maybe you should give it up, let it go up in flames: tit for tat. Because you're experienced, you've already done this, you've actually felt the wall of heat, the rain of ashes, heard the explosion of ignition, the roar of combustion, the pop of fire meeting glass. You know, everything can blow: Your provisions of clay, your hothouse lights, your antenna-repairing tools, your juice-concoction recipes, your Monopoly and Trivial Pursuit games, your midwife accessories (what might they be?), your flea-foam-bath and Tender Vittles, your pizza delivery truck, the stained green sofa you left in the alley for a scavenger. To ashes: tarot cards you could've read, vegetables you could've served while brainwashing a new customer, lawns you could've mowed, journals you could've burned yourself in the kitchen sink, business cards you printed on a letterpress in a graphic arts class in college and could've distributed when you started a business, poems you could've painted in calligraphy on velvet unicorn paintings. But anyone who's a musician in this game, especially a gifted musician who was out earning a living wage on the day the fire card is drawn, their ax doesn't burn. They still have everything they need. They win. The others might learn their lesson. They might win too, next time. They might learn what's important.

1986

The report from Ed Meese's pornography commission was released in a two volume set for $35. Included in the publication was a lengthy listing of book, movie and magazine titles such as *Teenage Dog Orgy, Cathy's Sore Bottom*, and *Lesbian Foot Lovers*, as well as several hundred pages of specific descriptions and excerpts from the listed material.

Change the World

It was around then Home Depot opened less than a mile away. It was the first one Marcy had seen. Someday it would be torn down because it was too small. But back then, it was the most enormous hardware store anyone had ever imagined. Bigger than Handyman, than Builder's Emporium, than Dixieline Lumber. It went in where an old FedMart had been standing empty, so not everyone was worrying about big box stores accelerating sprawl, although Marcy voted for the no-development candidates for city council.

After being married five years, Marcy and Kurt had bought a house. By changing little things in their lives and routine they'd been able to save the down-payment. She prepared meals from raw, fresh ingredients, and packed Kurt's lunch – cream cheese, walnuts and sprouts; or cheese, lettuce and tomato sandwiches – instead of him going out. She repainted the furniture she had in her apartment, some of the same stuff her mother had gotten from the Salvation Army thirty years ago. She and Kurt shared the 1979 sub-compact car Marcy had bought in the first year after graduating high school, and she put all of her bank teller salary into a money market account then just paid the bills with Kurt's paycheck. To stretch his salary, they also seldom went out to a concert or movie, never went on vacations, hadn't even had a honeymoon, except African nut soup at The Prophet, their favorite vegetarian restaurant – decorated with portraits of Mohamed, Confucius, the Dali Lama, the Maharishi, Rama, Lord Vishnu, even Jesus.

Their real estate agent had complained once that a client had looked too long at her legs instead of at the houses she was showing. Marcy giggled about that, later, to Kurt, because the woman had chalky-white legs the size of baseball bats. Still snickering, Marcy had speculated aloud whether the woman's sexy legs would help her make sales. Kurt merely suggested, "Maybe she knows how to use them." After closing escrow, the agent gave them a gift coupon from a home-improvement catalogue. Marcy said, "At least she's not offering you her legs," and chose a socket wrench set. Her father had never gone anywhere without his, and an extra one had always sat open on the coffee table.

On one side of their new house, the neighbor had a pile of rocks just about filling her back yard. The houses were built with their back yards against a little hill made of sandstone with smooth, globular rocks mixed in, as though this was close to the river, which it wasn't. Some freak of geology caused the hill to continually spill into the neighbor's backyard. Marcy planned to put ice plant groundcover on the embankment above her yard. Their piece of the hill wasn't falling, but it was bare, with hardened gullies of erosion.

The other neighbor had weedy grass a foot high, shaggy oleander bushes growing through a rusty chain link fence adjacent to Marcy's driveway, and a cinderblock wall separating the two backyards. But their street ran downhill, so the weedy neighbor's back yard was higher than Marcy's, and the cinderblock wall that was over Marcy's head in her yard only came up to her neighbor's waist in his (just as the wall on the other side of the yard only came to Marcy's waist and she could look down into the yard full of rocks). The weedy-lawn neighbor also had a dog who put its front feet on the cinderblock wall and barked, with spit flying, every time Marcy went into her own back yard.

Kurt didn't notice these things because he didn't go into the yard. He practiced his Tai-chi and his electric keyboard and previewed promotional record albums inside the house. He was manager of a Wherehouse record store. So he was indoors the Saturday the police visited, after Marcy called them. Marcy had been in the yard trying to figure out what she should do about the places in the lawn that were just bare dirt because half the year they got no sun. (Sowing more seeds wouldn't do any good. She thought some sort of raised garden bed where she could grow vegetables, with park-like benches mounted on the timbers enclosing the garden.) The neighbor with the dog was actually watering his scrubby grass and disheveled bushes. He was also smoking and tossed his butt into Marcy's yard. Marcy retrieved it and went to the wall, holding the cigarette up toward the man as though passing a smoke up to a prisoner in a second floor cell.

"Please don't toss trash into my yard. This is still smoldering, it could've caused a fire."

"What?" the man replied. It looked like he might have no teeth.

She held the butt even higher. "Don't throw your cigarettes into my yard!"

The man turned, and his hose turned and squirted Marcy in the face.

The police, who arrived alarmingly quickly, spoke to the man, then knocked on Marcy's door. Kurt had to turn down Miles Davis or Chuck Mangione, Marcy couldn't tell them apart, although she did her Jazzercise to one of them.

"I don't think there'll be any more trouble, ma'am. He says it was an accident."

"He tossed a burning cigarette into our yard."

"He's just an old alkey," the other cop said. "We'll drive past a few times in the next half hour. He'll calm down."

"Alkey?" she'd asked Kurt, after the police left.

"Alcoholic." He was cleaning the record with special solution and a dust-free cloth. "Didn't he remind you of anyone?"

"Not particularly."

"Your father?"

"My father's not an alcoholic."

"Well, you should've called the police on your father, not our new neighbor."

"*You* didn't do anything."

"Do what? About *what*? Your father? I didn't even know you then." Kurt didn't look at her, slipping the record into its sleeve.

"No, you could've gone out and *said* something to . . . the old alkey."

"Say what? About what?"

"He squirted me with the hose. It was no accident."

"So stay away from him." He pulled another record out of the stacked wooden grocery crates that exactly fit record albums. "Leave the yard alone, leave the grass alone, leave the hill alone, don't try to teach the neighbor manners. Why are you always trying to change everything?"

"To make things better."

"Better than what? Why can't things just be what they *are*? Why can't you just move into a house and live in it?"

"You mean don't fix anything?"

"Who's saying it needs fixing? Broken things need fixing. Leave everything else alone."

Marcy decided to put up a fence against the cinder blocks that would be high enough to block the dog and his owner from looking into her yard. ten-foot high fence boards would do it. Nail the fence boards, side by side, to two parallel sixteen-foot 2x4s – one 2x4 securing the fence boards at three feet from the bottom, the other 2x4 fastened three feet above that. Then stand the fence up flush against the cinderblock wall, and just pound six-foot metal stakes into the ground on the other side to keep the board fence upright. After that, she would undertake the raised vegetable garden surrounded by picnic benches.

Her father never hit her, never laid a hand on her. He also didn't drink, no more than anyone else. He went to work, came home. He drove a cement truck for a while. Then other kinds of trucks. Gravel trucks, trucks delivering dirt here, picking up dirt from there. The things trucks did. If she still knew him, he could help pick up and deliver the railroad ties she would use to make the raised garden bed. But the last time she'd seen him was the day she'd arrived home from junior high and found her clothes, her shoes, her stuffed animals and caged rat all piled on the front lawn. Her dad had decided it was time for her to move in with her mother. If it hadn't happened, she wouldn't have met Kurt, because her mother lived a hundred miles away, with her new husband. It was too late to imagine her parents would ever get back together anyway, but someday her father surely would have to at least explain.

Kurt was three years older, a senior when Marcy started high school. He was in the band. Marcy was in the drill team that followed the band down the street, making crisp synchronized motions with white-gloved hands, the metal taps on the heels of their white boots clicking in unison. Their school mascot was a yellow jacket, so there wasn't much of a ready-made costume, except yellow and black. They'd worn tailored miniskirts, yellow with black inside the pleats. There was an alternate uniform that was black with yellow instead the pleats. She hadn't really known Kurt then, just knew who he was because he was the band's president and marched with his trombone in the center of the front rank. She and Kurt didn't start dating until Marcy was a senior. Kurt came back for the homecoming football game. By then Marcy had quit her position as captain of the synchronized-hands marching unit and joined a boycott of the whole homecoming queen ritual. She was picketing outside the football stadium, carrying a sign that said *Cow Auction Today* and chanting *Hey-Hey,*

Ho-Ho, this big boob contest has got to go. Kurt was in a little group of former band members who tried to drown them out with Sousa marches.

Apparently sparrows lived inside the Home Depot, it was that big. They flitted and chirped in the metal rafters overhead. Marcy was looking up as she wheeled a clunky lumber cart that never put all four wheels on the ground at the same time. She'd already loaded twenty-four ten-foot by eight-inch cedar fence boards and the two sixteen-foot 2x4s. As she was pausing over at the bins of nails, adding in her head, an employee passed, directing a customer farther down the aisle toward metal screws and bolts. The customer was someone Marcy knew. It was Colin, a boy from high school. Not just any boy, but her boyfriend in the tenth and eleventh grades. She knew it was him even though this man was getting fat. His pants were too tight and he had a gut straining against a t-shirt over his overly-western belt buckle. His face was wide, his nose was broad, his head was enormous. His hair was considerably shorter than in 1978, and the blue on his face where he shaved was only on his chin and upper lip. In high school Colin had grown a fringe-like mustache, and Marcy had been glad when he'd had to shave it off for the two months of band competitions. He played the snare drum in marching band and tympani in the school orchestra, which replaced marching band as an elective in the spring. Colin had liked a girl who played cello as much as he liked Marcy, so he alternated between the two of them, for two years going with Marcy during band season, and the cello girl during orchestra season. In eleventh grade, when the band and auxiliary marching units visited Disneyland after their last tournament of the year, Marcy had shoplifted a knit hat from a gift kiosk when Colin did; she thought if she didn't, it might be his excuse that year to break up with her so he could go with the cello player during orchestra season. At first Marcy was only choosing one of the longshoremen's hats because Colin was getting one. Then when she turned toward the cash register, he'd said, "Are you going to *pay* for it?" He'd balled his hat in his fist and turned to walk away, so she'd followed. They'd gotten caught. A grim plainclothes security guard led them to an office down a concealed alley off Disneyland's main street where they sat opposite a desk from another man, the shoplifted hats on the desktop along with some of the other junk they'd actually bought, like some sort of stuffed lizard from the Tiki Hut. The lizard stood on his mangled wire-manipulated feet with his mouth open and teeth showing, facing

Marcy, and she just stared back at it, tears gushing, Colin hunched beside her, while the man reamed them and said he was calling their parents, but as far as Marcy knew he never did (unless he called her father by mistake). On the bus ride back, Colin and Marcy hadn't spoken. They'd sat crushed together in the back of the bus, Colin's hand in Marcy's shirt, rhythmically squeezing one breast, and Marcy still wept every now and then because she knew he would break up with her for the cello girl anyway, and he had, after not seeing Marcy at all during Christmas break.

It's not that Marcy thought about Colin once a week, even once a month, hardly even once a year in fact. But when she did, she had wondered if Colin would someday contact her and apologize for the shit he pulled in high school. Once when she'd mentioned that idea to Kurt, he'd laughed and said it would keep the post office and phone company in business indefinitely if everyone apologized to everyone they'd fucked over in high school. "Well, *I* would, if I'd jerked anyone around," Marcy had said.

"How about those girls trying to be homecoming queen?"

"My right to free speech."

"You threw mud on them."

"I did not!"

When he saw her, Colin said "Hi," but not a surprised haven't-seen-you-in-years *Hi*, just Hi. His smile didn't exactly exclude his eyes, but didn't include them either. Colin was half-Japanese and his almond eyes could be vacant when he stared dispassionately – like the times he broke up with her, or the time she didn't want to try his mother's seaweed-wrapped rice rolls – but she thought they had squinted merrily when he smiled, although she couldn't remember a specific time.

Colin's pants were too tight for him to put his hand in his pocket. He wedged his fingers in up to his knuckles, shifted his weight to one leg. Marcy was wearing overalls. She thought she might've had them since high school, but she could be remembering her painter pants, which she'd worn at a few school events, like the Earth Day rally, at which they'd chanted, *All we are sayyyying . . . is give hemp a chance,* and carried signs that said Hemp, not Trees. They'd also spread dirt over part of the quad, to protest the paving of America. She'd loaned the stuffed lizard from Disneyland to a boy who had a sign that said *Ours to Protect, Not Destroy.*

Colin was wearing his inscrutable mask, the same face he wore the time he'd been absent from school on December 7, and when he came back the next day some boys started calling him Tojo. It was probably near the time Colin would be breaking up with Marcy after band season, so she hadn't said anything back to the kids who were ragging on him.

"So . . . you building a . . ." Colin examined her lumber cart, ". . . paneling a room?"

"No, just a fence. A piece of a fence. Long story. I live near here, do you?"

"I moved to Riverside. But I own a rental house in Linda Vista. Needs some rain gutters."

"Wow, you own an extra house? It would've been weird if we'd ended up renting from you. We finally bought a house, Kurt and I. Kurt Carlson, remember him?"

"I don't know anyone from high school anymore."

"Me neither . . . except Kurt, I guess. I didn't know him then. But you would know that. Hey . . . whatever happened to, you know . . . she played in the orchestra. . . ?"

Colin's expression, which maybe she was learning to read again, waited for more information before he finally shrugged. And as though giving in to someone pestering for a life story, he said, "I met my wife at work. When I was a security guard. Then I finished my associate degree and got a real estate license. I have three kids."

"Already?"

He didn't smile. He also didn't ask if she had any, so maybe it was obvious she didn't. The Earth Club in high school had some Zero Population Growth literature, and she'd mailed in a postage-paid card joining a mass-pledge not to have children. Before she got married, she'd been saving her money to get her tubes tied, but when she made the budget so they could save for a down payment, her savings all went into the house account. Not that it mattered that much anymore. Marcy and Kurt hadn't had sex in over a year. Sometimes she wondered if Kurt wondered what had happened to them, or what he thought about when he thought about it, or if he used Tai Chi to forget about it.

Colin cleared his throat, then said, "So . . . did you ever become a lawyer?"

"A lawyer?"

"Didn't you want to be a lawyer?"

"When?" she laughed, "before or after my life in petty crime?"

"You're kidding."

"No, you know . . . Disneyland. . .?

What was on his face . . . confusion? Marcy felt hot and looked up into the rafters. The sparrows were twittering contentedly. It had become part of the Home Depot white noise: forklifts beeping, paint-shaking machines ratcheting, shoppers droning, lumber carts groaning, squeaking, banging . . . sparrows singing. A bird paused on a box of deadbolt locks on the top shelf of the aisle, in its beak a few bristles, perhaps from a broom or a paintbrush.

"Nesting." As Marcy spoke, the sparrow fluttered higher, into the roof beams. "Like us. We were going to change the world."

Colin was watching her, not exactly staring, but as though she was growing an extra eye and that's exactly what she was supposed to do, and what he expected.

"Well . . . time to go make lunch for Kurt, or he might succumb to the smell of frying fat from the McDonald's on the corner. Want to come see my house and have a bite to eat?"

"No thanks. I've got some guys waiting to install gutters."

"Okay. You might not like radish sprout salad and miso bean soup anyway." She looked down at the box of nails she'd been holding all the while, remembering she only had peanut butter and cracked wheat bread at home.

Marcy had been a vegetarian since before going to live with her mother. Secretly at first, because her father still wanted beef or pork with every meal, and since fourth grade Marcy had cooked his dinners for him. But she'd taken a vow against meat when she was ten, the day her father squashed her new kitten under his truck tries in the driveway then took the mashed carcass and fed it to his dog. Kurt had been skeptical about the vegetarian diet at first, but curious, in that everything-you-do-is-interesting mood of a first date, which involved an Italian restaurant. By then she had also renounced white sugar, white flour and preservatives, which made an Italian restaurant difficult because of the pasta, but she could have the eggplant parmesan. Eventually Kurt had been easy to convert, especially after he discovered Tai chi.

"By the way, I like sushi now. Actually just the taki — rice rolls with vegetables, I don't eat fish. Like what your mother made, that time when I wouldn't eat it. . . ?"

"Did you meet my mother? I lived with my father and stepmother."

"She was Japanese."

"So is my step-mother."

"But who made the taki—rice rolls—that time?"

"I don't know, what time?"

Colin didn't have a hand cart or shopping basket, just several packages of something in one hand. He started to move down the aisle, but slowly, not walking away from her. "Are you going to pay. . . ?" Marcy asked from behind, before she caught up. A clunk from the lumber cart before she could finish with the word *now*.

"Yeah, this's all I need. We started the job but were missing just a few bolts, so I ran over."

Marcy was trying to get the lopsided cart to roll not-too-unevenly as she walked beside Colin. He was going slowly, as though to accommodate her efforts, but he went into a ten-items-or-fewer line, so Marcy checked out at the next register, a little surprised to find him waiting for her when she was finished, an orange Home Depot bag balled up in his hand. He didn't grab a hold of Marcy's lumber cart, but again walked slowly beside it as she maneuvered out the sliding glass doors to the parking lot. Just outside the door an employee checked their receipts.

Marcy started to laugh, but when Colin's small eyes still just gazed like shiny opaque stones out of his overly large face, she said, "Am I going to be able to guess your car from the bumper stickers?"

It turned out his car was a station wagon with a *Baby On Board* sign suction-cupped to the rear window. The car next to his—one of those tiny old Hondas that several boys could pick up and move from the parking lot to the sidewalk in high school—had a *Nuke the Whales* sticker. After graduating from high school during the second oil embargo, when people lined up for blocks to buy gas, Marcy tried to go without a car. She'd already answered a roommate-needed ad in a weekly newspaper and moved in with a girl who turned out to be a born-again Christian. But the school Marcy went to that summer, to learn to be a bank teller, was across town from her new apartment and class started at eight a.m., so she'd bought a used Datsun that promised forty miles per gallon and made payments on it for a year. It was still their car—Kurt dropped her at work on his way—and her only bumper sticker was a fading *Carter/Mondale*. She and Kurt had been dating during the 1980 election, and Marcy had participated in door-to-door blitzes for the Carter campaign. She told Kurt if Reagan won, she was moving to a different country. On election day, she and Kurt were messing around on her bed with the radio playing an FM jazz station. She'd gotten off work at four and it was around five, not really dark yet, just almost. Suddenly the radio was announcing

Carter's concession. "No!" Marcy had yelped, vaulting off the bed, "Wait for me!" Fortunately they weren't undressed yet. She and Kurt had run across the street to the VFW hall where the local polls were still open. When she remembers it, she thinks maybe they were both zipping their pants as they dashed into the voting booths. The next day, she'd dropped her purse into her drawer, slammed it with her shoe and announced, "Well, I'm moving to Canada." The other tellers looked up, most of them just airheads, bank robots—ATMs hadn't threatened anyone's job yet. That night when Marcy's roommate was playing her Christian quasi-rock in the living room, Marcy and Kurt huddled in her room and decided to get married and rent a house so they wouldn't have to share walls with anyone who might have that or any other unsavory taste in music.

"Well . . ." Colin said.

"Yeah, nice running into you."

"Yeah, I gotta go."

Marcy was shoving her lumber cart up the parking lane, not very far away yet, and Colin called, "Hey . . ." Marcy turned, bracing her weight to keep the cart from rolling back toward Colin. "I know why you were confused," he said. From that distance, his eyes were still just black spots, his face large and looking clammy, like he'd actually broken a sweat but hadn't noticed it yet. "My father got back together with my real mother. But wait, I think that was after high school. I can't remember. The only thing I cared about back then was not turning out like him."

After only a slight pause, Marcy said, "You did a good job."

Kurt had made his own peanut butter sandwich and went to his Tai-chi lesson in the park. His note said, "I can make it there in time on the bus, if I leave now." She thought he might call for her to pick him up, but they didn't have a cordless phone, and Marcy spent the afternoon making her fence, and luckily the spitty dog must have been locked inside. The hardest part was getting it to stand upright against the cinderblock wall by itself while she pounded the metal fence posts into the dirt. Also, the ground wasn't all that even, and in some places the bottoms of fence boards grinded into the dirt, at others they hovered above, not touching. Something about where the weight was distributed, and which part was absorbing the most pressure, was off, but it was standing there, blocking the neighbor from looking or spraying his hose or throwing anything into her yard, and blocking his dog from barking at Marcy.

Kurt had called and left a message saying he was going out after class with the instructor and few others. He didn't say so, but Marcy knew they went out for tea, not beer, and talked about chess and another game called Go.

If Kurt had been there when she'd gotten home with her lumber, she would've said, breathlessly laughing, "Guess what I found out about my high school boyfriend!" If he'd come home while she was still hammering nails or setting the fence upright, she would've snickered, "I saw my ex-boyfriend at Home Depot and guess what, he's fat." If he came home now, as she sat in the living room sipping orange juice, she might have said, "I saw an old boyfriend in Home Depot today." She finished the juice and went to take a nap.

The sound that woke her was, at first, like a thunderstorm. A loud crack. A thump on the roof. Two more thumps. Another crack. Some of the other commotion was unspecific, and she could hear the old alkey neighbor's voice, but couldn't make out any words, as though he'd taken out his dentures and was having a fight with literal flapping gums. But an argument with who? His fleshy blousy wife who wore shapeless Hawaiian-print dresses, but who actually bothered to have a job? There was no second voice, but perhaps the other half of the argument was inside their house, and it was boomeranging back-and-forth to the outside, and the fallout was raining on the rest of the neighborhood. The front screen door bashed then shimmied for a second. More muffled thumps on the roof. Shattering of glass on concrete. Two, three, four more snap, crackle, pops. Bumps on the roof, and a vibrating, booming crash, like a gong, on the metal covering over Marcy's patio. Once during a halftime show, the band had played the 1812 Overture, and a special percussion section had been wheeled onto the field—huge base drum for the cannon blasts, a gong for the explosions, chimes for the church bells, while off the field someone had tried to time fireworks to detonate at the right place in the music. Now as she tried to hum the melody of the 1812 Overture, to fit with the racket outside, Marcy remembered she had slipped a black glove over one white one, then raised her fist and left the football field in protest over the glorifying of war for entertainment, although the Earth Club had voted not to stage a demonstration that night since they needed to get student government money for their rain forest float in the homecoming parade. (After Marcy walked off the field, the faculty leader of the drill team had told her she was being replaced and suspended for a week, but Marcy decided that when she walked off, she had also, right then, quit her position on the team and as captain.)

Everything became quiet, and Marcy was counting inside her head. She got to a hundred, then two hundred, and it was still quiet. But she closed her eyes, waiting for more. The war in Vietnam had been over by the time Marcy got to high school, and not a single boy she knew would be drafted or go overseas to a battlefield, but she was thinking about Vietnamese villagers caught in the crossfire between Vietcong and American forces, hiding in their huts, counting the seconds between burst of shelling. But then again, the village was never just caught in an unfortunately located battle; the village *was* the battle, the village was the target.

Marcy padded in her socks through the living room, into the kitchen. Through the kitchen door window she saw a brown beer bottle in three pieces on her concrete patio. Two more brown bottles, whole, on the dirt in the yard that should be growing grass. Then, off to the side closer to the alkey neighbor, she saw a broken piece of wood . . . then another, then another. Her whole fence was smashed, many of the upright cedar fence boards splintered off and tossed into her yard. The rest, a jagged snarl of fractured boards twisted askew but still attached to the 2x4, lying flat, with more broken bottles glinting among the kindling.

Marcy backed up, squatted on the kitchen floor, breathing hard but not crying. If she could've called Kurt, she would've. But this was before cell phones, before pagers. Long before e-mail and chat rooms and instant messaging. Before Columbine and Oklahoma City and OJ. She crawled back to the bedroom, shut the door and turned off the light, started a fan to create white noise, to drown out anything else she might've heard. And without sleeping, managed to not even hear Kurt come home until he flung open the bedroom door, demanding, "What the hell's going on? There's dogshit by the front door. Someone threw dogshit at the house."

"Dogshit *too?*" Marcy whispered.

"Yeah, it's all over the driveway."

"It's more than that," Marcy said softly, without moving, without turning toward Kurt. "The neighbor, he broke the fence I made, he threw bottles and trash into the yard. He went on some sort of rampage."

"You had to go and stick up a *fence?*"

"I told you why."

"Yeah, and *now's* when we should be calling the police, but we can't –
he did this *because* you called the police."

"I was only trying to give us some privacy in our own yard."

"I don't go in the yard. I don't care about the yard. How about what
happens here, in *here*? How come you're not obsessed with fixing what
happens, or doesn't happen, in *here*?"

Marcy rolled to her back and looked at Kurt. He was very thin, had
always been thin. He had narrow shoulders and a lean face. Once at a
bank party, when someone said he was lucky he could eat whatever he
wanted and not gain weight, someone else teasingly asked him if he'd
been a POW. The two people had both been women.

"Please, Kurt, could you go pick it all up? I can't bear to look at it.
Please. . . ?"

Kurt left, and over the fan Marcy didn't hear anything. Until, after a
while, she heard the refrigerator open and close. She heard the mumble
of the television on the other side of the wall. On Saturday at five there
were reruns of Kung Fu. Grasshopper still wandered around the old West,
spreading quiet wisdom, having women fall in love with his unflappable
self, never succumbing to temptation, although she had wondered aloud
to Kurt once, snickering, whether he boffed every one of them, but it just
wasn't part of the storyline.

When Marcy came out to make something for supper, she peeked
into the yard and didn't see any debris.

"What did you do with the dogshit?"

"Trash."

"What do you want for dinner?"

"Some of that dogshit sounds good."

"Want to just get burritos from the place on the corner?"

"I thought they had lard."

"Can't be any worse than dogshit."

The following week, on Saturday afternoon while Kurt was at Tai Chi,
Marcy was taking a bag of indoor trash to the cans on the driveway, and
the old alkey neighbor was in his front yard, again with a hose. Her
trashcans were around the side of the house nearest his. The bags of beer
bottles and dogshit had departed with the trash pickup that week. Curbside
recycling wouldn't begin for another year or two, so the beer bottles had
gone into the regular trash. Ordinarily Marcy would have insisted they

keep the bottles and pieces of bottles separate and drive them over to the recycling center near the landfill, but she didn't say a word when the glass had clinked like chimes inside the bags as she carried them to the curb. The stack of splintered fence boards had been too much for one pick-up and was still on the side of the house beside the cans, waiting to go into the trash little-by-little.

Marcy put her head down and started to skitter around the side of the house, but the neighbor called out, "Hey . . . hey, c'mere." Without his dentures again, his words as spitty as the dog's bark over the backyard cinderblock wall. Marcy looked up. The man gestured for her to come closer. He was wearing one of those pleated-down-the-front shirts, like a dentist smock. His salt-and-pepper hair was thick and longish, but lank and stringy. Marcy was coming nearer as slowly as she could. He gestured again, then dropped his hose. "C'mere, I want to show you something." Every 'S' blew out some spit. Kurt had warned her not to antagonize him again. "Come around," he said, so she did, coming around on the side-walk to his front yard, and when she got there he was holding a shovel.

"I got something I want to give you," he said. "I'm so ashamed for what I did. I got something to give you."

"You don't have to give me anything."

"What I did was terrible, I want to give you something."

As he spoke, he was going around the side of his house, on the other side of the same cinderblock wall where Marcy had put her fence, but here it only came to her waist. She stopped to see how her yard looked from up here. It was a fairly complete view of everything: everything she'd planned to fix but hadn't yet, the dirt where grass should be, the bare embankment that could come sliding down, and the top side of the metal roof over the patio where she saw a faded green frisbee and a deflated rubber ball that looked like a stomach. There were also four more brown bottles, several fist-sized rocks, and some grayish looking things that were obviously turds.

"Look there," the man said. Marcy turned away from the startling view of her own yard. The man was pointing with his shovel to the dirt beside the foundation of his house. A skinny rubbery plant was growing all alone there, with a few thick leaves and a long neck supporting one dark bruise-colored flower. "It's a black lily," he said. "They're very rare. You dig it up and take it to your yard."

"You don't have to give me this."

"Take it, because I did such a bad thing. I know I did a bad thing."

Marcy stared at the lily because she didn't want to look at the man's toothless mouth or the sweat starting to ooze from his hairline. She groped for the shovel and he put it into her hand. The dirt was hard, but she managed to get most of the shovel under the lily, in a circle all the way around, until the lily with its roots in a dirt-clod were on the shovel, and she carried it home that way, then passed the shovel up to the man over the cinderblock wall. She dug a hole right there, beside the cinderblocks and planted the black lily. Its neck was flaccid and the flower sagged to the ground.

Marcy never built the raised garden surrounded by picnic benches. She did put flagstones down where the lawn was mud, and she put a flower trellis up against the cinderblock wall, with a fast-growing jasmine to block the neighbor and his barking dog. But the neighbor shot his dog one night, the sound of the gun making Marcy bolt upright in bed while Kurt never stirred. Later that year she would sit naked in a hot tub—at a former downtown motel remodeled to rent out dayrooms with saunas and Jacuzzis—beside a supervisor from the bank. She kept washing her mouth out with the chlorinated water between the times she went down on him, because there wasn't a lot of information on whether oral sex was safe. She wanted to be promoted from teller. The following spring she was living in an apartment, alone, and the house had a *For Sale* sign when the black lily would have been sprouting again. On her last trip moving the last of her stuff, which Kurt had packed and left on the porch for her, she went into the house to leave a note for him. She didn't know what the note would say. She eventually left without writing it, but before that, she went through the kitchen and out to the yard to check the dirt beside the cinderblock wall for any sign of the black lily.

1987

A television commercial for condoms aired in San Francisco was then banned from broadcast.

Michael Jackson, who had purchased the entire Beatles music catalogue two years before, attempted to purchase the bones of the Elephant Man.

Our Time Is Up

The word, that year, was *co-dependant*. Barb was in a co-dependency group. Too young for a *midlife crisis* (that, believe it or not, was from 1965), but was exactly where she should be to begin probing the concerns of *adult children* (1983). *Yuppies*, identified in 1984, had already discovered if their families had been *dysfunctional* (1981), and were ready to become *empowered* (1986) but first would need co-dependency therapy. They wouldn't *reinvent themselves* until 1989 and couldn't find their *inner children* until 1990.

Barb was only half-listening when the counselor began her opening speech at the first meeting. Besides Barb there were three other women. Somehow Barb had already learned: MaryPat was a waitress who used to be something else. Gloria was loud and flamboyant, newly divorced, and Barb didn't know what she did. Belinda did something in an insurance office and had two pet rabbits and a husband who traveled a lot. The counselor had been seeing at least two of the other women alone, and had recently decided to have group sessions. So when Barb had been calling the numbers

. . .you may deplore the behavior—it may hurt you, terrify you, drive a wedge between you and your spouse or child or parent; it might make you feel hopeless, helpless, frustrated, angry. But are YOU helping to keep, to maintain the trouble in your relationship? Are you addicted to the addiction? If you do anything to assist the addicted person to get through his or her day, you are co-dependent, and you are ENABLING. You're assisting them to continue their

listed in the phonebook under counseling, this was the first one who'd said she had an opening in a new group for women she was starting. How was Barb to know the counselor held sessions in a small bedroom converted into an office in her apartment in one of those old neighborhoods near the park where a jet had crashed a few years after they'd moved here, the type of place where everyone was a vegetarian and still wore their graying hair long and parted in the middle and didn't shave their legs and let their horny toenails show through leather sandals while they were holding group counseling. And it took over an hour to get to San Diego from their condo in Del Mar, so she'd had to miss her afternoon aerobics class and sit in Friday afternoon gridlock to get here. Who had group therapy on Friday?

dependence—that is, allowing the condition to continue and even to get worse. If you grew up this way, being co-dependent to an addictive parent, your dysfunctional family experience trained you that this is the only way to subsist, to co-exist in a relationship, and so you will likely be co-dependent in your adult relationships. It is only by breaking the cycle that you can experience a healthy, supportive relationship.

After she had found the group, but before the first meeting, last Saturday morning, Bobby found her where she was reading on the pool deck. He was holding a folded newspaper and said, "I know you like dance movies. There's a new one, let's go see it."

She'd looked at him and almost said, "Don't try so hard. It hurts." But she went to the movie with him. It was *Dirty Dancing.* Near the beginning, Bobby leaned over and whispered, "They can't be serious, a character named *Baby?*" Afterwards he said the movie had reached new levels of cheesiness.

There are other expressions of co-dependency besides enabling an addict. Much of it stems from low self-esteem. You may have been abused or neglected as a child. You may be someone who will decide what to do based on how much it will please others.

Barb bought the soundtrack, the next day after work. Bought it on LP even though they were trying to switch, but the album had a larger picture of Patrick Swayze than the cassette or CD. Before Bobby came home, she made a cassette and put it in her car, unmarked. Bobby would never notice the album, slipped in between *Flashdance* and *Fame,* to the right of WHAM ("Take Me Out Before You Go-Go"). Tuesday afternoon, she asked the aerobics coach to use her *Dirty Dancing* tape, even though she knew exercise tapes had to be custom mixed so all the tunes were the proper speed:

warm-up, build-up, aerobic peak and maintenance, through warm-down. *Dirty Dancing* had all different tempos, and they came in movie-plot order. Growing up, learning about sex, falling in love, then profoundly changing someone's life didn't necessarily happen in the same progression as heart rate during aerobics class. So she listened to the cassette going to and from work, Wednesday and Thursday, and going to work this morning, and on her way to group an hour ago.

Barb was on a sofa with compressed cushions, the brown plaid fabric pilled and scratchy. Belinda was beside her. The counselor was in a scratched dining-table chair to Barb's left. This put the counselor's bare toes closest to Barb. Gloria sat in another dining chair facing the counselor, and MaryPat, on a vinyl avocado green ottoman, faced the sofa.

You may only be able to feel good about yourself when you are helping someone or listening to a friend describe her problems. Then if you're in a situation where you need help, you may turn away from help, feel uncomfortable receiving that kind of attention. You may appear to all the world as a competent adult, but you're so focused on what others need and how you can please them, you know very little about how to direct your own life.

Barb's husband didn't drink, smoke, gamble, or do drugs. Both sets of their parents were still married, hadn't ever beat them or their siblings, hadn't tried to have sex with them, hadn't neglected them at Christmas or birthdays, came to their school plays and band concerts, likewise didn't drink, smoke, gamble, over-eat or do drugs. Couldn't you have all that and still be unhappy?

Now Gloria was talking: *. . . to be for the first time only responsible for mySELF, and I'll tell you, it's so empowering. I even enjoy doing my laundry and cooking my dinner. I'm the one deciding when to go to bed and when to get up—at least on weekends. Weekdays I still have to be at work at 7 a.m. But I'm going to start applying this whole concept to my boss too. I've enabled him to be disorganized because he knows I'll keep track of everything, I'll never let him miss an appointment or lose a file or forget to pay a bill. I guess it's made me feel important that he needs me so much, so now I understand: I'm co-dependent to the scatterbrained contractor, and believe me, he is addicted to his own organizational incompetence because it makes him feel more important. HE does the creative or*

Barb was deciding what she should say when it was her turn. How much would be enough? Start where she and Bobby moved here from Terre Haute in 1976 the day after he graduated from ISU with his engineering degree? Neither of them even had a job, and within four days of arriving, amid the unemployment of the late '70s, she'd started making appointments and checking patients in at Dr. Easly's old office in Santee. Bobby found his job a few weeks later, a civilian company with contracts from the Navy, but he'd moved from that job, and had moved several other times before finding the one he stayed with, designing recycling machines for a local company that sells them to municipalities and waste management companies (commonly called *dumps*) all over the world. . .But that was really getting off the point, even though Bobby's cutting-edge work would make the rest of these women's husbands or exes look like redneck meatballs, but that wasn't really the point either.

Someone else had started talking. . .

important thinking and decision making, I'm just the dull administrative assistant who can only think in daily details. But as soon as I stop enabling, I'll be out of that cycle and can empower myself with other kinds of value. That book just absolutely changed my LIFE. Like when my ex tried to come in the house last night, claiming he needed to get his tools and it was part of the agreement—I wouldn't let him in. I'd changed the locks. When I'd made this so-called agreement, I was still being co-dependent, allowing him to bully me into getting his own way just because it was easier than fighting. So in my mind it's invalid.

It was MaryPat: "But . . . if you didn't make appointments and file . . . I mean, isn't that your job?"

"It doesn't have to be who I am."

"So I serve drinks to drunks. It isn't who I am, and it doesn't mean they've forced me to be a waitress. I chose to be a waitress because I make a hell of a lot more money than when I was a junior high band teacher."

"MaryPat," said the counselor, drawing her sandaled toes back underneath her dining-table chair, "is there some subtext you'd like to share?"

Yeah, we were both music majors, and we both wanted to be band directors, but all along, now that I look back, they were aiming me toward junior high while it was always understood he would have a high school. And that's exactly how it turned out. Bruce was Mr. Important field-tournament-band-director, bussing to Los Angeles, to Phoenix, to Santa Barbara for tournaments with his entourage of equipment trucks and band parents wearing some kind of their own uniform, horning in on their kids' high school life, coming home with trophies, blah, blah blah, while there I was teaching Mary's Little Lamb to eleven year olds spitting into trumpets for half the pay. Well, not HALF, but not even three-quarters. So I quit and went back to waitressing

Barb is trying to listen to this one, but she honestly can't imagine how anyone could care if their husband's dumb band got some trophy and yours didn't. Bobby makes model cars and little radio-controlled airplanes and sometimes comes home from his weekend shindigs with a plaque or a ribbon, and Barb didn't start complaining it was a chauvinistic plot. She could give a flying flip about his little cars and airplanes, really, even though he tries to show her the minutest details on them (sometimes she has to just pretend to be seeing what he's talking about).

and now I make more than him, but obviously I work nights and we barely ever see each other, especially weekends when his buses have to leave the school at around five a.m. to get to whatever tournament they're doing. And when he gets home, he expects me to have waited all day just to find out how well his band did. If I don't gasp with enough awe, he gets cranky, and there's another evening we barely speak.

"So you're enabling him to outdo you by quitting and letting him be the star," Gloria said, shifting her butt and re-crossing her legs as she spoke. Like Barb, she hadn't changed from her skirt and pumps before coming to the group, but Gloria's nylons looked too glossy. "You're actually addicted to being second chair."

"I just said I make more money than he does. I just can't always be saying oh-you're-such-a-wonderful-high-school-band-director-honey with any real enthusiasm."

"Maybe you're greeting him with other kinds of you-messages," the counselor said. "You should concentrate on using only I-messages. Do you know what that means?"

MaryPat shook her head, so the counselor started explaining. Barb felt like she was falling into the crushed sofa, like her butt suddenly weighed twice as much. Which is often what happened when she missed aerobics. Friday there was jazzercise after aerobics, and Bobby always stayed at his office Friday afternoon, having a beer with his partner and waiting for the rush-to-weekend traffic to pass. There was never any reason to believe it wasn't what he was doing. Until he surprised her a few months ago. But she's not going to start there. Is it

You-messages can easily be, and often are, accusatory, even hostile. Why did you do that? You're making me feel worthless. You were late. You're being insensitive. You're not being fair. You're spending too much. You're the one who thought we should buy this. Most people will get defensive when receiving you-messages, and then a useful communication will be impossible. Try I-messages instead: I feel sad that this is important to say that they met while Bobby was in college, but she wasn't a student, she just happened to grow up in Terre Haute? After she graduated from high school, she started right away as a key punch operator at Fieldcrest Industries.

happening. I'm trying to understand why you're upset. I'm sorry you feel that way. I'm worried about our money. I-messages invite the other person to communicate, rather than shut the doors to communication.

She'd been working there three years when she met Bobby, and went on working there after they (secretly) moved in together before they got married. She'd cried the night of their wedding, but not the tears-of-joy weeping girls did in the novels Barb read; she'd never done that kind of crying and didn't know why—what was wrong with her? That night Bobby had asked her why she was crying and all she could think of was, "I just never thought I'd get married." Was that an I-message? They were all practicing their I-messages.

"I feel I'm ready to participate more in the business," Gloria said to her contractor boss.

As if any contractor was going to ask his secretary for construction advice — like how many nails he would need, how much cement?

"I'm sad that my plans to be a band director got wrecked," MaryPat said to her band directing husband, "and yours didn't."

"Should he apologize for that?" the counselor asked.

"Okay—I'm sorry that you think I should be happy that my plans got wrecked and yours didn't?"

"You don't *sound* like you *chose* to be a waitress," Gloria said.

"That's a you-message," MaryPat returned. "Besides, a waitress is almost a self-sufficient private contractor. It's one of the few things women have if they want to be independent."

What a ball-bender, that's what Bobby called women like that one.

"I don't like spending so much time without you," Belinda said to her traveling husband.

Another would be prostitution.

"Have you said that to him?" the counselor asked.

"Yes. I think so. I don't know."

"Or did you say, 'why do you have to leave me alone so often?'" Gloria asked.

Who's the counselor here anyway?

"Maybe. I don't know."

"What does he say?" the counselor asked.

How about GET A LIFE?

"If I say anything about it, he gets real quiet and goes to watch TV or sits in his study. He says traveling is what makes him like his job so much. He bought me the rabbits so I wouldn't be alone."

"Long-eared rats are no substitute for a husband," Gloria said.

"Why not a dog?" MaryPat asked.

"They don't allow dogs in our apartment."

Are there enough I-messages in that one?

"I'm going to get a dog," MaryPat said. "I think I want a dog with papers. I want to show it."

"I think that would be good for you," the counselor approved. She turned toward Barb. "We haven't heard from you yet, Barb."

While Barb is talking in group therapy, Bobby is still in his office at the recycling machine company, with Carl, the other engineer, having a few beers and waiting for Friday rush traffic to dissipate. It's September, so they talk about football. The Chargers haven't lost enough games to be out of contention yet, but the baseball team was a lost cause months ago and aren't worth an exchange of two sentences, except to bemoan how the Chargers have to play with a dirt infield outline on their football field grass until the baseball season mercifully ends at the end of the month.

One Friday Carl had brought Wild Turkey and they'd done shots, and Carl had the brilliant idea to call a guy he knew in the manufacturing unit who knew how to contact a girl who would come over and give blow jobs for fifty bucks. They did, one at a time, in the engineering office, while the other sat just outside. Bobby had never had a blow job before, but he didn't admit it to Carl. Barb said asking a woman to do it was demeaning to her, not just because you're asking her to put his body's waste-emptying conduit into her mouth, but because he could experience the whole thing without once touching her, and, in fact, it was like he could be alone, watching TV while he got it. He didn't know how it was much different than the hand jobs she gave him to "take care of him" when he was horny and she wanted to go to sleep. She didn't use the word *conduit*; she probably made up some medical-sounding word, which she was prone to do at parties when she made pronouncements about vitamins or nutrition and he saw people exchange glances. He took a long time to come because he did feel weird about it, coming in the girl's mouth, but she wasn't being paid by the hour, and Carl didn't say anything about how long he'd sat outside the door; he'd already had his turn.

About a month later, Carl brought up calling the girl again, and he still sometimes suggested it, maybe once a month, but Bobby always said, "We don't have anything stronger than beer," and Carl let it drop. Bobby had already told Carl about his worry that something was going on between Barb and someone at the doctor's office she worked at—not the doctor, but someone like a doctor. Barb had said it would take too long to explain what a PA was, more than a nurse and less than a doctor, she'd said. As though he was some geek with his head up his butt.

Since they do this almost every Friday, Bobby doesn't bother to tell Carl that Barb is at her first group therapy meeting. It had been her idea to go. While she'd been deciding, and vacillating, he'd tried to be encouraging toward whichever way she chose, individual, group, or none at all. She'd been dramatically listless—at least when he saw her, at home—since that night three months ago. He didn't know what she was like at work. He couldn't imagine how she would describe that night, or what else she might be saying tonight, like what was going on inside the house in Tierrasanta that he had waited outside for over an hour. After Barb had come out of the house and walked past him—giving him only a startled look, and maybe even saying "hi," (*hi*? as though they were meeting on a campus between classes?)—he'd gone straight to his office, this office. Another time that he sat in his office, long after working hours were over, except without Carl, and without a girl giving him a blow job. He'd already had Kathy's phone number in his wallet. He'd had it for a few weeks, since he'd called information in Terre Haute. He sat for a while before calling. Kept hearing Barb saying "hi," but not really sure if she'd really said it, or maybe *he* said it. Maybe he was the one who said it, from the darkness under the tree he stood beside, and that's when he'd seen her surprised look.

While everybody looked at her, listening, Barb said,
I don't know how it happened . . . it just . . . I don't know . . . happened. I met someone who . . . listened to me, thought I was funny and . . . I don't know . . . smart . . . He understood the things that worry and bother me, and . . . talked to me about what worried and bothered him. With him, I

felt so . . . I don't know . . . more myself . . . like I was myself for the first time in my life. And I . . . But I . . . couldn't be with him because . . . I don't know . . . he was engaged. . . . He'd been engaged for so long, but wasn't married. . . . He'd been married before, but . . . I don't know . . . that doesn't matter. . . . He lived alone. Lives alone. He . . . Sometimes I . . . need to talk to someone . . . about things. . . . Just things that . . . I don't know. It had been three months. One . . . or two days a week . . . I went home with him, instead of to my aerobics class. I needed it. It was something I . . . I don't know . . . had never had. Then . . . it wasn't right for him, for Bobby to . . . follow me like I was a criminal . . . and spy on me. . . . I don't check on him when he stays after work and drinks with his buddy. He told me what they do and I believe him. I don't remember what I told him . . . I told him something . . . he should've believed me. . . . I might have said I need to do something . . . that I needed to. . . . It was something I needed . . . to do. To do for me. If I didn't . . . take care of myself . . . like my aerobics. . . . I . . . I don't know. . . . But anyway, he followed me . . . I don't know how long he was there. He was standing outside when I left. Just standing there in the dark like a secret agent. When I told Hal, the next day at work, he . . . later he said we needed to . . . stop. The shit hit the fan for him too, he said. Just like that. His fiancé was getting uncomfortable and asking questions, he said. It was . . . so easy for him . . . to say it. So easy for both of them to just . . . I don't know . . . tell me I can't have . . . what I need.

She wasn't looking at them anymore. She picked at a little loose ball of nylon on her knee.

She wasn't going to tell them what she and Hal did. It would desecrate it to reduce it to words. They were the most beautiful, sheer, breathtaking, alive moments of her life—that's what drug addicts probably said, but she didn't need drugs—but she wasn't going to give it away by trying to explain.

From where he stood in the dark outside the PA's house in Tierrasanta, Bobby had gone directly to his office in Chula Vista, which was the opposite direction from the condo in Del Mar. But while he'd stood outside that house in the dark, on the parkway beside the sidewalk, under a tree that rained some kind of pollen or seed shit he later found in his hair, what had he thought about? Sometimes Barb asked what he was thinking, and she didn't like his answer: that he was hungry, that his football team was lousy, that he was too tired to get up. That night, if she'd asked instead of walking past, he could've said he was thinking about how they periodically found old World War II munitions buried in backyards or empty lots in Tierrasanta, because during the War it had been an empty Navy testing ground, far from any populated areas, and now it was in the middle of a city, a whole community with a name that meant Sacred Ground. Bobby had learned some Spanish before moving to California because he'd heard it could help you get a job. He'd learned from tapes, listening to them over and over during the drive from Indiana—he drove the U-Haul and Barb the Datsun—and also had practiced by looking up in a dictionary the English translation for all the town and community names. *Of the Sea . . . Hidden Valley . . . View of the Ocean . . . View of the Plateau . . . Beautiful View . . .* and just plain *Beautiful.* So he'd gotten curious and wondered what Terre Haute meant. It was French and meant High Ground. So, standing there in Tierrasanta, he'd thought about coming from high ground to sacred ground.

He made the call from his office in Chula Vista, which he hadn't been able to translate with his little dictionary. A view of something. His dictionary, still on his desk, said Chulo meant pimp. That was weird. He hadn't thought about that for a long time, not even when they'd called the girl to give blow jobs. She had been a Mexican girl, and that had troubled him. He'd become the Ugly American. With Kathy, he had only kissed her and touched her large breasts through her sweater or blouse, and yet it had been far more exciting than his first blow job.

It was almost nine o'clock in Terre Haute. It would be ten o'clock if it weren't daylight savings time, but Indiana didn't use daylight savings.

Kathy answered. A simple, uncomplicated "Hello?"

"Hi," he'd said. "It's . . . Bobby."

"Pardon me?"

"Bobby. Bobby Winston."

"I'm sorry?"

"Remember . . . from high school?"

"Oh."

"I'm calling from California."

"Oh. . . ?"

"I moved here after college. I guess I haven't talked to you since before that. I don't remember the last time we . . ."

"Oh, Bobby."

"Yeah, it's me." His voice almost a whisper.

"I'm sorry, I guess I haven't thought about high school for so long."

"Yeah, me neither. I got married and graduated and moved . . . Or graduated and married and moved . . . I don't remember. So, how are you? You didn't get married? I mean, your number is listed with your last name, I remembered it—"

"I'm divorced."

"That's good." He swallowed, blinked hard. "I mean, maybe you can tell me what *that's* like . . . I mean . . . it's hard, being married. Isn't it?"

"Why are you calling, Bobby?"

"No reason. Just to say hi. I just thought I'd see what you were up to."

"Why? That was high school. I've been married, divorced. Then I made a clean break from that part of my life. I'm born again. I can't be taking calls from another woman's husband."

"I didn't mean . . ."

"Goodbye, Bobby."

There was a moment of silence. Barb wiped her last tears. She was holding a Kleenex she doesn't remember taking from a box beside her. She looked up, and then they started:

Oh, wow, been-there-done-THAT . . . I've been the one picking up the phone and hearing it disconnect. I've been the one wondering why it takes so long for him to drive home from his job fifteen minutes away. I've been the one finding the Virginia Slims cigarette box in his car, the one wondering why his

Not looking at them anymore, again. The loose ball of nylon was now the start of a run from her knee to her thigh. Not sure she's still breathing.

court shoes are still at home but he said he was playing basketball after work, the one crying myself to sleep because of that bastard and his current floozy. Who's the co-dependent here? Maybe your husband needs co-dependency therapy, he's the one not divorcing you after finding out you're cheating. HE'S enabling YOU . . .

How could I expect you to understand. Rabbits really are the perfect pet for you.

I would never do that. I could just never do that. Randy's away from home so much, but . . . I could just never do that. That's . . . just something I could never do.

Are you sure you're in the right group? I mean, maybe it is my fault I gave up, and it galls me that Bruce's band is winning all the time, but . . . to go behind his back, to have an AFFAIR? That wouldn't be my answer. And believe me, it wouldn't be difficult to find someone, in my line of work. But that's just tacky. It sounds like a soap opera. It sounds like the drama is what you're after. Like coming here and crying is part of the whole deal, and you like it as much as the sneaking around and cheating. Is that it? Didn't you ever ask yourself IS THIS ALL THERE IS? You yuppies—isn't that a Beemer you drove here in?—what's the UP for you anyway, what do you WANT?

You're right, this is obviously the wrong place, the wrong group, the wrong . . . oh god, why did I come here?

Barb, maybe we need to hear about your feelings in a different way. What did you want from the group when you shared?

She could hear herself answering, and the questions came from everywhere, the know-it-all, the surly ex-band-director, the rabbit girl, the hairy-legged counselor. She didn't remember the kleenex box moving to her lap. She kept hearing herself answering, but she was thinking about getting into that BMW which seemed to have made the band director so angry—or even *more* angry—and start driving and keep driving, all the way back to Terre Haute. She'd had such a cute studio apartment there, near the campus, near the football stadium—she should tell MaryPat how she could hear the drums and knew when it was halftime—until she'd meet Bobby, a student living across the hall with 2 other guys, then somehow her cute apartment was gone and she was living beside the train tracks with Bobby, in a building filled with college kids, a place she'd been glad to leave for the adventure of moving to California. And now. . .

"I don't know."

No, I think MaryPat meant what were her upwardly-mobile goals?

"To be . . . To not have to work someday. For my husband to . . ."

What—did you want to have children and stay at home and have no financial independence? Why didn't you go to college?

"I don't know."

Why don't you have children?

"I don't know."

You say that a lot.

Did you ever ask your husband about it, Barb?

"I don't know. I think so."

What did he say?

"That I never said anything so he never said anything."

Didn't he want children?

"I don't know. We liked the way things were."

Then why are you unhappy now?

And why did you cheat with someone else's man?

What *had* she wanted, ever, once upon a time or even a year ago? And why had she moved here? Because Bobby had been preparing for four years and had decided, before he met her, to get out of Indiana and go somewhere where the things an engineer did could matter to the world. The day after graduation, that's what he did, and by then she was beside him, packing a U-haul long into the night. That had been ten years ago. Did she ever wonder, that night, if she were single, would she have chosen this? But what *else* would she have done? Before she met Bobby, what did she think she'd be doing in a year, in ten years? Had she ever given it a single thought, or was the naive pleasure of paying her own rent and arranging her own things in her single room and buying her own bag of groceries once a week too much of a giddy drug? But once here, she'd become comfortable, immediately, with things she enjoyed: walking on the beach, especially in the winter when the threat of burning into blistered, peeling red paint was past; or her jazzercise classes with other women who tore the neckbands out of their sweatshirts; or the condo's pool where she read a book every week, even though Bobby called them *rescue-me-fuck-me* books. Hal liked her to read to him.

"I don't know. It just happened."

That's what addicts say, they don't take responsibility. You could've just said-no.

Is there an AA for soap opera addicts who try to live like they're in one?

I read they have CoDA organizations, a 12-step group, I guess we're not a big enough group for that kind of thing?

12-steps are religiously based, but here we can support each—

Coda is a music term, a passage at the end of a piece or movement that brings it to a close.

It's for Co-dependants Anonymous. So let's bring our co-dependency to a close. Your band can play a symphony when my boss realizes I'm not a doormat.

I don't have a band. Doing your job isn't being a doormat.

Not getting credit for it is. Isn't that why you quit?

I changed jobs.

Tomato tow-ma-to. You should at least tell him the real reason you did it. You should get the book, really, it changed my life.

Girls, I think our time is up.

Girl, as a pejorative, never earned the horrific level of *boy*. In fact, just the opposite. It even became *girl power* (1986), while *boy*, racist undertones notwithstanding, at best was limited to its *toy* rhyme-ability or connotation, as in *game boy* (1989). An adult male did not want to be a *boy*, but could be a *New Man* (1982) which, near the end of the decade had disintegrated into a wimp or *wuss* (1984). Being a *girl* was better than being *wimmin* (1983, a spelling to remove the word *man*). While *girl* hadn't yet become *grrl* (1994, but not an attempt to remove the *I* from *girl*) the pretty, gentle word may have helped women feel younger, even pleasantly vulnerable. Or less alone, as in *girlfriend*.

Barb never went back to the group, and she quit her job at Dr. Easly's office, even though she might have become office manager someday. Bobby either didn't notice or didn't comment, until she told him she found a better job at a hospital doing outpatient and emergency room billing. He said, "That's good, you'll probably get some additional computer training." Doctors never came into the office where her desk was, where she kept a picture of Bobby beside her telephone, and a magazine cover of Patrick Swayze in her drawer.

One day, when Bobby didn't want to figure out how to use the coffee maker, he was going to boil some water for instant coffee and found a video tape hidden in a pot in the cupboard. Of course he played it and found an interview with Patrick Swayze on Entertainment Tonight.

Meanwhile, there were always new words. For example: The *virtual reality* (1987) of rush hour traffic is that *road rage* (1988) is like a dance movie *from hell* (1987) where you can't tell *moshing* (1987) from *wilding* (1989).

Bobby came home one day and went directly to where Barb was reading on the pool deck and told her he was moving out. Barb cried for what seemed like three days straight. There was no one to ask her why. She had to pretend Bobby was dead, like Patrick Swayze in *Ghost*, and had told her he'd love and protect her forever, and was hovering near her every moment, looking over her. When Bobby started seeing someone, Barb told him she was dating a doctor named Patrick. But eventually Patrick had to leave to open a clinic in . . . Paris. Of all places, Paris needed a free clinic with a handsome American doctor named Patrick. Barb could've started a Patrick-Swayze-anonymous group—PSA, like the airline that had fallen from the sky, just a few years after they'd moved here from Terre Haute, and exploded not far from where the fading hippy counselor held co-dependency therapy.

1988

Asked about the Holocaust, Dan Quayle called it "an obscene period in our nation's history." Reminded that the Holocaust did not take place in the United States, Quayle explained he meant "in this century's history. We all lived in this century."

My Husband's Best Friend

She ordered meatball soup. There was one meatball. I said it was a bull testicle. I couldn't ruin her appetite.

We were there to talk about: My search for a career across the continent, her lover 2000 miles away waiting for a commitment. My husband wondering if being married was what he wanted, our new unintentionally similar haircuts, her budding friendship with my husband. Also: my memories of being fired from a job I loved, her anger at her brother for giving her a nightgown for Christmas, my childhood remedies to prevent my body from maturing, her new stock portfolio that she tried not to audit every day, my husband's recent curiosity about sex with two women at once. And maybe something else.

We shared a chocolate mousse. I carefully shaved the pudding with my spoon in an upward motion. My side looked like Half Dome. On her side she plunged in and ate whole spoonfuls at a time. I gave her the cherry on top. We stopped talking for a while, sat looking around. The waiter kept filling our coffee cups. My fingers were trembling; I switched to decaf. I wished I would stop handling everything so well, just go ahead, fall to the floor, twitching, foaming at the mouth. Things were winding down. Then she took my hand.

They'll Shoot You

This decision should be as easy as resolving to avoid dangerous places. She's going to tell him about it tonight.

Cici watches Jeremy's eyes move across hockey statistics in the newspaper. His mother has told Jeremy, in private, that Cici could use some cute new clothes to wear instead of jeans. Jeremy told Cici later. He also told her his mother had informed him—as though it took her a day and a half to do the subtraction—that Cici was eleven years younger than him. His answer: "So?" He was mean to his mother. Cici told him that in private. He laughed. "She needs to be kept in line," he said. "She might want me to start visiting more often."

He has decided that they'll leave for the hockey game three hours early, eat at the place where two larger-than-life hotdog people—one a girl, the other a boy—stand on the roof, then go to the game, walk around the inside of the stadium looking at the souvenirs, try to sneak down close to the ice to watch the warm-up, then find their seats, after the game go to Greektown for gyros.

"That stadium's in a bad place," his mother has said, just a minute ago. "They'll shoot you down there."

Cici had looked at Jeremy and he grinned back at her. "They will," he said, "every time you go."

Now his mother says, "The roads are icy."

"Maybe we'll be killed skidding off an overpass and you won't have to put up with us another three days."

"Oh *you.*"

Cici keeps looking at Jeremy because after three days she won't be able to look at him anymore for a long time. He sticks out his tongue or crosses his eyes or makes a wildman face or grins a manic grin or smiles gently, sadly. He has lovely hazel down-turned eyes and sweetly crooked front teeth.

Long before this visit, Jeremy had told Cici over the phone, "My mother cries easier than anyone I know, except you. The biggest difference is that she can also stop on a dime. She might say five sentences, the first one she's normal, the next two she's crying, the forth and fifth she's perfectly normal again, just bossy as usual, as though nothing happened."

"What does she cry about?" Cici had asked.

"She misses my father, she wants to see me more often, she's worried that Glenda will kill me."

"Does she cry when she tells you not to get married again?"

"No, that's when she's bossy. She's bossy about 90 percent of the time."

Just before the first time Cici had to leave Jeremy in California for what was then her new job in Cincinnati, he'd suggested she get a new car for the long trip, strongly recommended it, advised it, called around and found the lowest price on the type of vehicle best suited for her needs, forced the dealer to get it in the color Cici wanted. Tears gathered in his eyes the morning she left, his nose red and slightly transparent. She would've reached to touch the tears beginning to run down his face, but he held her too close, put his chin over the top of her head. She knew he wouldn't shut his eyes but would keep staring over her head around his garage. That's where they were. Finally he'd whispered, "I guess you better go." That was over a year ago. Since then she's had to leave him again and again, after being together a week, a month, three weeks, a weekend, two months. This time it's just five days together—all five at his mother's condo in the Sauganash neighborhood in Chicago, two thousand miles east of his house in Del Mar and Cici's currently uninhabited apartment in San Diego; eight hundred miles northwest of her rented room in Cincinnati.

"All set for hotdogs, hockey and gyros?" Jeremy says. He already has one arm in his coat.

"It's hours early," his mother says, "You don't need to go yet."

"We'll take a drive." He turns his back on his mother, rolling his eyes for Cici's benefit.

"It's icy," his mother says. "You should listen to the traffic report. You should take a cab."

"I drive better than a cab driver."

The few times it snowed in Cincinnati while she was there, Jeremy reminded Cici over the phone to drive slowly and make every motion smoothly: turning, braking, accelerating, everything.

"Why is it icy?" Cici sighs. "It's supposed to be spring. It *must* be spring. It's the middle of March, so it's supposed to be spring."

"Welcome to Chicago, baby."

He lets his mother's Buick fishtail down the street on the ice while Cici squeals and grabs his arm and shrieks "No, don't," laughing. Just before the busy cross street, he purposely skids and slides almost sideways at the stop sign, opens the window and shouts "Free at last!"

Now Cici's position as a seasonal botanical consultant at the Cincinnati Zoo, March through November, will probably be eliminated. When she'd first described her job to him, he'd asked if they would ever send her into a lion's cage or the wolf enclosure or a bear's habitat to inventory the flora or check damage to trees. A certain smile, showing his eyeteeth, means he's joking. At a traffic signal, looking at a burned and boarded-up house, imagining it new with the trim painted and flowers in the window boxes, people on the front porch waving as holiday guests leave on July 4, Cici says, "They may offer me a full time position instead. Twelve months instead of nine. I'd be there year-round."

"What? When did you find that out?"

"Last week."

"Why didn't you tell me?"

"I'm sorry. I was thinking about what I'm going to do."

"So, what're you going to do?"

"I don't know."

"You sound like they offered you terminal cancer instead of a job."

"That's exactly what they offered me."

Over dinner, she tries to smile at him with her mouth full of hotdog, onions and relish, not knowing what it looks like since it feels like a grimace with a lump in her throat. Like cancer. When it grows, it makes her cry. When she cries, it gets bigger. "You look like you really needed this," he says.

"Yes, just fill me with carcinogens and preservatives, I'll live forever. You don't have to worry about me."

When she had thought she might get a bicycle to keep in Cincinnati, he'd said he would worry about her getting hit by a car. When she wanted to take horseback riding lessons in Kentucky—something to stimulate her senses when she was away from him, she'd said, only partly joking, the heavy scent of horse and hay, pastoral beauty of a Kentucky farm, the warm solid feel of something alive between her legs—he'd said he was afraid she'd fall or be kicked or bitten. That time he hadn't been smiling.

She doesn't cry until just minutes into the game when two players fight and one comes away bloody, sent to sit alone in the penalty box and wipe his blood on a used towel. "It's so stupid," she sobs, "they ought to be ashamed."

He laughs. "This place is sold out, and you're the only one crying."

"But the babes with big hair snapping their gum aren't going to cry."

Finally the player throws away the dirty towel and bursts out of the box. "What should I do, Jeremy?"

"I don't know what to tell you." No longer laughing.

It is cold in the stadium. She keeps her coat on and hugs herself. She'd almost left her gloves in the car, glad now that Jeremy had suggested she take them along, just in case.

All the cars had been parked side-by-side and end-to-end, a solid mass. Those fans earliest out to the lot sit idling, blowing steam, until a space breaks in front or behind. Jeremy tries to slide across each frozen puddle that isn't already cracked or smashed, some no larger than the length of his shoe. His mother's white Buick is still surrounded. "Chicago cars," he says, pointing to two of the closest ones with rusted-out fenders, dinks and dents, hanging mufflers. He'd told Cici to wash her new car once a week, especially during winter in Cincinnati, because of the salt.

The motor running, the heater on, he says, "I wish we were going back to a motel instead."

"Or home," Cici says. "I mean . . . San Diego."

"I know." Sometimes his voice is so gentle, her insides kink up.

Last month when she left San Diego to return to Cincinnati for her spring contract, he'd said, "It's kind of fun, think of it that way, you're important, you're the only one who can do what you do, so they have to bring you in several times a year."

"I'm not the only one."

"But think of it that way, it'll make it easier, they need you."

"What about you?"

"I'll be okay. You'll be okay. We'll be okay. And when you come home, you can find a different apartment, okay?"

"Why? I hate moving."

"I don't like your neighborhood. I'm worried about it. It's changing. There's all those robberies and shootings and gang activity less than half a mile away. I worry about you at night, sometimes. Aren't you scared to sleep there?"

"I sleep there, what, 10 percent of the year?"

"More than that."

He'd told her to tell repairmen and door-to-door salesmen that she's married but her husband isn't home at the moment. He wanted her to somehow imply to the landlord that she was married or that her boyfriend was there most of the time.

"Why?"

"You can't tell what they'll think or do if they know you're living there alone. And *never* tell anyone you work out of town half the year."

"It's more than half, Jeremy."

Something hits the window beside Cici, a dull thud like someone's elbow or head. The big backside of a man blocks the window for a second, then he gets into the car beside them. "Too bad we can't drive sideways," she says. But the car beside them doesn't move. The occupants get out again and sit on the hood, drinking beer.

"Don't look at them," Jeremy mutters, but the man on the car hood has begun gesturing, his voice coming through the windows as though he's far away, "C'mon, join us for a brew, wut's yer hurry?"

"I already smiled at him by accident," Cici says.

"Uh-oh. Why'd you do that?"

The owners of the car on their other side have arrived, two more young men, but they don't leave either, just sit on their car's hood and trunk, swinging their legs and kicking the sides of Jeremy's mother's Buick. The first two men are right up against Cici's window, pressing their faces there, kissing the glass, their lips smashed like the underside of snails or slugs. The other two shout greetings and toss beers to three more guys arriving from the stadium who go to the cars in front and behind. One sits on the hood of the Buick. The others lean against the Buick's white fenders.

"What's going on, did they plan this?" Cici asks.

"Probably, when they got here."

"Why us?"

"Maybe because of the car looking so new, and it's a fucking *Buick*. Maybe just random."

On either side, two guys are tossing opened beers back and forth. Large splotches splatter the window like vomit.

"Jeremy. . . ?" Cici kneels on the seat, her back to the window. "Maybe . . . could I, maybe . . . instead of a new apartment, maybe I could move in with you . . . I mean, when they eliminate my part-year position. I'm not asking for a free ride, it could save us both, I'd pay rent to you. I'd find some kind of job, I have lab experience, or I could teach intro to Biology at night school, I'd landscape your house, work at a nursery, I could even be a gardener, mow people's lawns."

"What about the full time thing they offered?"

"That's only a maybe. But you know what it would mean."

"I know."

The car starts to rock. Two guys in front and two guys in back are pushing up and down like a railroad handcar. One guy is still riding the hood.

"Assholes," Jeremy says. He leans on the horn.

"Is there a security guard?"

"Are you kidding?"

The car continues rocking. One of the guys in back is standing on the trunk. "My mother would be dead by now," Jeremy says. "Or else she'd just be her bossy self and they'd leave." He pushes a button that sucks the radio antenna into the fender. "Look, Cici, you've got to do what's right and best for *you*, for your life. I don't want to sound like an insurance-company cliché, but you've got to be independent, plan for your future, decide what you really want to do that can also give you some security, and build your life toward it."

As Cici lowers her face to Jeremy's lap to dry her eyes on his leg, he hisses, "God, no, sit up, think what it looks like you're doing!"

"I didn't want to wipe my eyes, I didn't want them to think I'm crying because of *them*." But the car is suddenly still, all seven guys begin whooping and circling the Buick, pounding the windows with their palms, shouting, "Go for it, baby," "more, more, more!" "Eat it raw," and "deep-throat it, sweetheart, farther, farther!"

"Jeremy, have you ever thought about it, us living together?"

"I don't know, I like it the way it is now."

"With me gone *months* at a time?"

"Not that part."

"Do you *want* me to take the full time job in Cincinnati?"

"What I want can't enter your decision."

"But I've told you what *I* want."

The voices from outside are suddenly sharper.

"Hey, watch it," Jeremy says, "is your foot touching the window button?"

All the guys are piled on Cici's side, three or four hands coming through the window which has cracked open. Cici shrieks and lurches away from

Jeremy, both her hands on the window button, catching their palms and fingers in a vise or dull guillotine as the window strains to close itself, and their voices accelerate into painful howls, rough laughter, drunken shouts, "Let me in, you sweet bitch."

"Ow, goddamnit, I'll kill your boyfriend, I'll cut his balls off."

"Let's paaaar-tayyyyy!"

"Put the window down," Jeremy shouts, "Put it *down*," lunging across Cici for the window controls, "let them out, open it, *open* it!"

But Cici's thumbs are white, bent backwards against the button, the window's motor whining, the safety glass continuing to trap and hold the renegade fingers—still reaching for her while trying to pull back, perhaps becoming frantic, even panicked, but locked in place.

1989

Six days after he banned Pete Rose permanently from baseball,
A. Bartlett Giamatti died.

First Year in Meadville

No curtains on my office windows, un-frilled view through the storm glass, my feet on the ledge, chair tipped, head barely visible to those passing in the hall, remarking, "You spend a lot of time looking out your window." But I'm working, just like the man in plaid shirt and knit hat, still raking leaves in March. I watched him plow the icy sidewalks last month—snow turns to mud, but leaves don't go away. He's still raking. Maybe tonight his wife will press her face to his beard and inhale the scent of leaves and grass and oily tools and him, and their bodies will be lit like soft neon, like the brewery signs in Otter's where they'll go later for a beer instead of waiting at home for the scream of the phone somewhere past midnight, and neither will need a sleeping pill when they set the alarm, turn down the heat, sigh and shut their eyes, not afraid to lose their lives until morning.

Yes, I'm still working, feet still on the ledge, while a couple, holding hands, is leisurely strolling the sidewalk, stopping at an intersection to embrace and kiss—not passionately, no desperation, no time-panic although she turns off and he continues straight ahead. How can they walk in different directions, still visible to each other, not yet so very far apart, and not look back at each other? But they are finally out of sight, mine as well as each other's, and my heart beats in rhythm with the footsteps of yet another twenty-two-year-old boy striding along beside a girl, his hands in his own pockets, her arms wrapped round her own books. He bends forward slightly, turns to see her face as they walk. He has lots of hair, the solid body of a man, but yet doesn't know that in twenty years an ex-wife might say, "You were supposed to want to take care of me," never pausing to take a slow breath, uncross her arms from her chest, put her hands down from her hips, and realize that this boy might also wonder who'll want to take care of him, twenty years from now, when it'll again terrify and intoxicate him to walk with a laughing girl, wondering how and when to touch her, twenty years ago he never thought the second half of his wedded life would be sterile, this boy doesn't have a clue that in twenty years the woman he honeymooned with almost twenty years ago will say, "Maybe I stopped wanting sex because you were too small to satisfy me. I sucked dicks before I knew you—just not yours," this boy, this man can't imagine, can't know that in twenty years he'll still have the same frightening, confusing need for a woman to love his music, his movies, his laughter, his hockey team, his body.

But I had to leave and come to Meadville. I'm still working up here, the sun slips behind clouds and re-emerges. It's March and my first year is almost over. The scariest part is everyone says their first year, they did it too, spent hours looking out the window, without moving, as though dead. But not any more. And they're still here.

Cookie

She first encountered the neighbors on the steep adjoined driveways they shared. With an armload of letters, ad circulars and magazines from the mailboxes on the street, Nan's neighbor was making her way back down toward the houses on her white concrete half of the driveway, just as Nan was headed up her own black asphalt side to collect her daily barrage of junk. The neighbor was in her fifties, wearing a long cotton skirt, her hair in a babushka, and was accompanied by a child of around seven years dressed in purple shorts and a green sleeveless top. The family, Nan knew, were Eastern-European, but they hadn't fled poverty. The man was a contractor, had built several houses in the area, then he'd moved his wife and children into the one that hadn't sold, a monstrosity with a Sleeping-Beauty tower on the flag-lot next door to Nan.

Below the houses, a purportedly mafia-connected resort golf course meandered through bottomland, as though the native chaparral floor of a Southern California watershed had instead been flooded with a thick coat of green paint. Nan's lot, a carved-out level spot, was halfway up the canyon wall, overlooking one of the sea-level fairways. From there, her driveway was another steep climb to the road above. Called a *flag lot* because the perimeter shape of the parcel-plus-driveway was the outline of a flag and pole—with the flag completely unfurled in a stiff breeze. Near perfect privacy, except the flag lot next door whose driveway ran adjacent to Nan's, their flag extended the opposite direction, as if blowing in a different wind.

Nan had bought the lot overlooking the golf course with her inheritance, then built a modest house and dog facility. Six runs, a grassy exercise yard, small outbuilding with two rooms: one for crating, the other equipped for bathing and grooming. She bred, trained and showed Shetland sheepdogs, and was paid to train and show other people's dogs, often dogs owned by wealthy people who rarely had their animals at home.

Nan wasn't sure the neighbors spoke English, wasn't sure what to do, that day passing so close on the driveway. The woman gazed away, seeming to have eyes only for the tomato vines and squash her husband had planted on the strip of dirt bordering their driveway. But the child spoke up. "Hi!"

The child was chubby with a full moonface. Nan answered, "Hello."

"Hi," the child said.

Nan replied, "Hi, how're you?"

The child said, "Hi!"

"Helllllo there," Nan exclaimed softly.

"Hi!"

By this time Nan had passed the woman and child, but she turned quickly and looked closer, just for a second. Something definitely wrong there. The child clasped her hands together in front of her stomach, twisting her wrists back and forth like unscrewing a jar, fingers entwined. "Hi!"

It had been months before, when the European family first moved in, that Luke—the man who delivered drinking water to both Nan and the neighbors—had told her there was a husband and wife and several children, he couldn't be sure how many children, maybe a baby too. In fact, Luke thought another one could've been born since the family moved in, but he hadn't heard a baby in a while, those babies may have died. He said he heard, from someone on his route who'd bought one of the man's other houses, that there was one of those problems between the man and wife, both negative or both positive, one of those mismatches that caused some of the children to sicken and die or have other defects. He meant, of course, the Rh factor. These things didn't happen with dogs. Or if they did, perhaps it was one of the conditions that caused a bitch to absorb her litter while gestating, or caused her to eat the newborn whelps, or ignore them and let them die of exposure.

"Hi," the child uttered, and before Nan turned to continue her ascent to the mailboxes, she thought she saw the woman smiling, even laughing behind a dour face.

The rest of the way up her driveway, her own face burning, Nan couldn't help but remember a news fluff piece she'd seen the other day, a story about one of those child geniuses who'd graduated from college at fourteen and passed the bar at seventeen, ran his own law firm for ten years then decided on a career change and went back to college for a PhD in neuro-physiology. His mother reminisced that while she was pregnant with him, her doctor warned her the fetus could be born retarded. Was it a case of a medical opinion being wickedly wrong, or were there two equivalent possibilities at either end of a spectrum? Despite study and care in dealing with heredity, it still seemed such a grab bag.

Around this same time Nan's foundation bitch, Daphne, was pregnant with the litter that would contain her Best-in-Show / Champion *O'Nan Call The Wind Mariah*, a future Register-of-Merit dam of champions. Of course that day she didn't know how successful the breeding would be, and even though she endeavored to continually expand her understanding of genetics, her knowledge of the traits, good and bad, supposedly carried by both sides of the pedigree, it still seemed that all the possibilities, even probabilities supplied by the sire and dam, just swirled somewhere in chaos, like bingo balls in a big glass box, until the moment of conception, or the bingo lever is pulled, and random numbers—or haphazard traits of appearance and personality, proficiency and malady, strength and incapacity—are whisked up, called out and displayed, or manifested in whoever, whatever is finally born. You get what you get, that's all you have to work with, that's all there is to it.

Well, except the rhinoplasty her parents bought for her sixteenth birthday because, despite the blizzard of freckles and cloudy green eyes, despite the name O'Flannary, her original nose took a long bumpy trip down her face. Of course she also taped and braced her puppies' ears, the whole first year of their lives, to ensure a high, tight ear-set and perfectly tipped ear leather.

It wasn't long before Nan noticed, in fact heard persistently all day, the child next door repeating "hi," sometimes in the slow redundant rhythm she'd used on the driveway, sometimes a louder call as though to a friend across a restaurant, although still the same clipped monotone inflection. The rest of the time Nan could hear the girl bellowing, not words, just open-throated wailing or guttural cries. And she heard the other children, a few older girls, admonish her, "Maria, be *quiet*." Sometimes the utterances or shouts were muted, other times the child was obviously outside the house, and Nan easily discovered—because the only barrier between her nearly-private back lawn and the neighbor's yard was a small trellis of string beans on a corner of their property—that the neighbors had put the child out on their raised patio deck where a redwood fence railing kept her penned five feet off the ground, and the glass slider to the house must've been locked. The girl stood leaning on the banister, almost as though enjoying an afternoon or morning interlude overlooking the golf course, and called "Hi" to each group of golfers who passed. Most answered her, then when she repeated her short greeting, they answered her again. After her third "Hi," they might wave, or glance up sharply. By that time they were usually on their way again, heading down the fairway after hitting their balls a second or third time. They got into their golf carts and took a long last look over their shoulders, up the hillside toward the girl on the patio deck, still saying "Hi."

Nan planted a fast-growing eugenia hedge on the property line between her place and the neighbors, from the end of the driveway, alongside the house, ending where a steep landscaped embankment plunged down to the golf course. When Mariah was born, the individual eugenia bushes were only as tall as Nan, and the spaces in between each were as wide as the plants themselves.

Mariah was everything a dog should be. In fact, she was exceptional in every way and demonstrated her comprehensive quality from the get go. From the flashy full white collar, white up to her foreleg elbows, on the plume of her tail and a perfect triangle snip of white on her muzzle, to the deep sable red of the rest of her coat. From the sweet, merry expression of her dark, almond-shaped eyes, to the elegant length and arch of her neck. She was, in fact, difficult to fault: her muzzle full, her back-skull lean and flat, the angle of her shoulders laid back, her hocks parallel, her feet cat-like and round, her tail long enough to brush the ground, her topside level, her body shape cobby, her coat long and profuse, her teeth perfectly scissored, her movement at a trot swift and fluid with astonishing extension and flawless single-tracking. Add to all this a high-energy, confident, seize-the-day attitude that radiated not only health but spirit and vivacity. When Mariah was a year old and already a Best-in-Show Champion, Nan had to recognize that the limitations and faults in her first three dogs—including her foundation bitch, Mariah's mother—were sufficient to thwart their show careers, so she placed them in pet homes to make room for Mariah's more successful descendants.

Including other people's dogs who were being kept for showing or breeding, but not counting litters of puppies, Nan usually had at least six dogs requiring daily attention—cleaning and hosing down kennels, dispensing food (at least four different preparations due to special dietary requirements) and changing water, then basic grooming of all dogs, bathing as necessary (sometimes five or six before a show weekend), not to mention nail clipping, cleaning of ears, trimming hair on feet and ears, and dental cleaning. The dogs took turns out on the exercise lawn—certain pairs could be together, but many combinations were not possible—while Nan road-worked those being actively campaigned for championship points. She had a special bicycle with a fixture to which the dog was secured on a buckle collar, and she rode at a steady pace, keeping the dog at a trot for twenty minutes.

Nan's house had picture windows and glass sliders overlooking the resort. Outside the sliders, she had a few flowerbeds and one strip of lawn between her house and the steep downhill embankment. Separated from the dog facilities by her house, and finally separated from the neighbors by the eugenia hedge, it was a secluded part of her property where clients never came. But Nan sometimes went out there with Mariah in the evening, after the last of the golfers was gone, listening to ravens squabble with the hawks they chased from fir trees growing along the fairway whose tops were just about level with Nan's lawn where she sat throwing a ball for Mariah or just resting quietly while Mariah viewed her territory. If a late jogger came by, especially one with a dog, Mariah would growl low in her throat and stand at the lip of the embankment, neck arched, ears quiveringly alert, hackles raised. Her only breed-standard imperfection was that when guarding territory, when asserting her alpha position, she carried her tail straight up, a flag over her back. The profuse fur on her tail bristled out, and, combined with the abundant puffed-up hackles around her neck, clearly functioned to make her appear bigger to whoever she was warning away, so Nan hardly considered the gay tail a fault, it was natural and necessary.

After a few years the girl next door developed a second word, *cookie.* This could have been funny because all of Nan's dogs understood that word, although they didn't seem to respond to it when the girl bellowed it incessantly, inside the house and out on the patio deck, following her babushkaed mother up the driveway and back down. Nan herself used the word in the show ring, to bring the dogs' ears up and give them the necessary posture and presence. Sometimes, with a difficult dog who wouldn't show, she wondered if she shouldn't have named the dog *cookie.* But then, of course, the word's special meaning would be lost.

During the week, two or three people might have appointments to come by, to deliver or pick up dogs for showing and training, to have their show dog groomed (ostensibly to learn to do it themselves), to drop off a bitch to be bred or to look at a litter of puppies. They always wanted to see Mariah, or came into the enclosed kennel area and immediately spotted her, "That must be Mariah!" Mariah would be standing upright with front paws on the edge of her exercise pen, back feet hopping up and down, eyes laughing, her plume tail waving like a banner, as usual drawing every eye to see her first, capturing attention and not relinquishing it easily.

And yet, the consultation did often stray.

She was affixing a patch of adhesive moleskin to the inside of each ear on a four-month-old, then using yarn glued to the moleskin to draw the ears together, higher on the puppy's head, tying the yarn in a bow between the ears, and the puppy's owner, helping to hold the pup still, said, "What's with your neighbor? I said good morning and she looked away."

She showed a new owner how to line-brush: lie the dog on one side and start just behind the dog's ears, make a part down to the skin—a line—brush the long thick guard hairs and undercoat against the growth grain, then, by bringing more and more hair forward, brushing it smooth against the grain, the "line" will move further and further down the dog's body. This kept the wavy undercoat from matting flat, gave the whole coat its profuse, full bushy appearance. The owner said, "Hmmm, yes, I see." Then, "I think someone next door wants a cookie."

Nan tried to avoid answering her clients' extraneous observations, but when she did reply, she made every effort to keep her responses nonchalant and indifferent.

While Nan snipped off each whisker at its base on the muzzle of a young show prospect, the dog's owner, hovering too close and blocking part of her light, remarked, "Your neighbor's gardener gave me a long, hard look when I came down the driveway."

Nan said airily, "That's not a gardener, that's him."

When Nan took one dog onto the grass exercise area to train, the dogs remaining in kennels and crates in the outbuilding yelped a jealous, joyous chorus. Those who belonged to Nan could wear electronic bark collars, delivering a minor jolt of electricity if they made any noise while wearing the apparatus, but the collars couldn't be used on boarding dogs, and she no longer put one on Mariah, who was often free to roam the outbuilding and patio and walkway around the exercise yard. But almost every visitor asked about the other noise that Nan barely noticed anymore.

"Who's being killed next door?"

"What's with all the yelling?"

"Someone please give that child a cookie!"

"Is there something wrong with that kid I saw in the driveway?"

"What's going on over there, is that a T.V.?"

"There's a kid screaming next door, shouldn't you call someone?"

"I don't think that would help anyone," Nan said mildly. The consequences of neighborhood animosity could be, for a kennel owner, catastrophic. Antifreeze, for one—it was something everyone had, was sweet and attracted dogs, and was lethal. Around this time, Mariah had her first litter. Despite several serious inquiries from reputable breeders, Nan kept three of Mariah's first puppies and sold the two lesser-quality pups to novice clients who were interested in starting a dog-showing hobby.

Nan needed eight five-gallon jugs delivered every week because she only let the dogs drink purified water, but she'd been looking for a reason to switch water companies, since Luke had asked her to dinner or a movie. She'd tried the kind of answer meant to say no without having to say it directly. "I'm so busy, and I go to shows every weekend." But, if he found her around the kennels or in the outbuilding, if she didn't disappear into the house quickly enough when she heard his truck come down the driveway, he'd ask again if she had a show that Saturday.

"Every weekend," she smiled. "There's always a show somewhere. Even if it means I go five-hundred miles."

"Even Thanksgiving week, even Easter week?"

"There's no holiday big enough to deter dog-show people from our pursuit of points. It's crazy, I know, we have no lives of our own." She was standing with her back to the door, at the stainless steel sink in her outbuilding, washing all the aluminum water and food bowls in a basin of hot soapy water with bleach, then rinsing and setting them in a rack to dry. Viruses and bacteria were so easy to pick up at a show, no matter how hard you tried to keep the dogs' noses off the ground by carrying them from pen to ringside and wheeling them from the parking areas into the grounds still in their crates stacked on carts. Not to mention the dogs her clients brought, despite her requirement of a health certificate and certain extra tests, for giardia, for brucellosis, for coccidia, and other parasites, protozoa or bacteria that cause chaos in the animals' intestines or reproductive systems. Now was a good time for extra caution, with Mariah's promising offspring being grown out, and it looked like none of the three was going-off and losing quality.

"What are the points for?" Luke asked, pushing his dolly with the last two jugs through the door. "You win money?"

The room was more crowded than usual, with a pen for Mariah's six-month-old pups set up in the center. Nan dried her hands. "When you win, you earn points. Toward a championship."

"So how do you win? The biggest? The fastest? Or just the prettiest? Like Miss America?"

"No, not like that, they're judged against a standard," Nan said, unable to stop herself, even though it meant he was putting his clipboard down, leaning over to lay a ham-fisted rap on the back of a young bitch's head—the way you'd lovingly cuff a lab or Golden retriever. But the Shelties always ducked away and barked, they had no use for rough affection. "Besides," Nan added, "the Miss America judges would never admit they're using a standard, even if they are."

"How's that?" He squatted outside the exercise pen. The dogs came forward slowly, their cautious bodies low and slinky, then they stopped, braced, stretched their necks so just the tips of their noses almost reached the side of the pen where Luke was poking his thick fingers through the wire.

"A standard describes the perfect breed specimen," she said, counting while she poured daily heartworm pills from a bottle into her palm. "Shape of the skull and muzzle, angulation of the shoulders and hips, length of neck, ear set, tail set, shape of eye and foot, balance of length to height, texture of coat, everything about the dog structurally, overall appearance and minute details." The dogs in the pen stood up against the edge and licked their lips, muzzles straining toward Nan when she turned toward them with the heartworm pills. "Then there's the proper temperament—behavior and attitude—for each breed. The dogs are judged against that written standard."

Luke half-sat on a large crate with his thick thighs spread, his hands folded between his knees. His coarse black hair was slightly greasy and had only a few strands of gray. "So they have to win or they don't deserve to live?"

She knew he was kidding, but couldn't refrain from answering earnestly, "If they don't win, they just don't deserve to reproduce." Then Nan smiled when the young male yapped—as though in answer, but really was just aroused by the animation in her voice.

"Whew," he chuckled, "good thing *we* don't have a standard!"

She smiled again, but not at him. Mariah, trotting breezily with her tail up, had come into the building from the run area and dropped a tennis ball at Nan's feet. Didn't spook when she saw Luke. Didn't even give him a sideward glance. No need for his attention. Nan picked up the ball, watching Mariah's eyes glint and body brace in anticipation. "How do you know we don't have one?"

A lot of things had not measured up to the standard. Hadn't books and movies made sex seem glowingly, even cloyingly beautiful, all that burning and yearning, the slow tenderness and ardent pleasure of being the beloved. What it came down to had been a boy who took her home from high school and stopped somewhere, every day, to play a game that must've been called *See if You Can Get Out of This One* because that's what he'd said as he pinned her arms with one hand and half his body, used a knee to pry her legs apart.

From next door the invocation began: "Cookie!"

"Back," Nan said quietly, and Mariah took two steps backwards. "Tail," Nan murmured, and Mariah lowered her bush tail to her breed's correct carriage. "Stand." Like a tap dance, Mariah lifted and repositioned each of her four feet, almost too quickly to see, so she was standing foursquare, stacked and poised as she would be in the show-ring to show off her angulation and body-balance, her springy and durable musculature. She was rewarded with a toss of the tennis ball—Nan gave the release word, "Okay," as the ball arched high over Mariah's head, and Mariah jumped straight up, all four feet off the ground, to catch the ball in her mouth.

"*Cookie!*"

"There she is," Luke said, still in no hurry to resume his route, "The Cookie Monster. My daughter used to watch that on TV."

Nan paused from cleaning fur from a slicker brush, but didn't look at him. "You have a daughter?"

"Eleven years old. I'm divorced."

Was he waiting for her to say *that's good* or *how long*? Should she just ignore it or change the subject, or would that keep him there longer and seem like interest?

"Cookie!"

Mariah carried her tennis ball cocked in her mouth at a jaunty angle and trotted out the door with her tail back up. Behind her, Nan also walked toward the door—ordinarily an effective hint that a lingering visitor should do likewise. She paused in the doorway.

"Cookie! *Coooookieeeee*!"

"A human being who only says two words and knows the meaning of neither, would she know to go sit on a toilet when she has to go? I wonder." She'd spoken without planning to. Ordinarily the only direct comments Nan made about the child next door were offhand remarks to the dogs, like, "Do *you* want a cookie too?"

"Did you see, they got a visit from child welfare over there?"

"No. Why?" She took a step back inside.

"Shit—pardon my French—that kid's yelling all the time, who knows what's going on over there, they parade her up and down the driveway like nothing to be ashamed of, then I think they lock her up. Is she getting any help, any training, she's about the same age as my kid, I don't know what I'd do if she were mine, but . . . maybe some home for people like that, I know everyone thinks that's cruel, but what about the rest of the kids? Someone had to call the authorities . . . I'm glad someone did."

"But who *did*?"

"Well . . . whoever did, it was the right thing to do, they shouldn't worry about sticking their nose in. Like you said, who knows the whole story over there? If nothing was wrong, no-harm-no-foul, everyone just goes on with their lives as usual."

"I didn't say that. Now they probably think *I* called."

"So? What're they gonna do?"

"I think they . . ." Nan turned sideways at the doorway, how much more obvious could an usher-out be? "Uh, I'm expecting a client soon, so maybe you'd better move your truck . . ."

"Yeah, I'd better get to my next stop. Maybe next week you'll find a night when you'll want some dinner?" He winked when she moved aside to allow his dolly room to get out of the door.

After Nan switched to a new bottled water company, Luke had come back once and rang the doorbell. All the dogs in the runs and in pens in the building sounded off with rapid-fire barks, including Mariah who now lived in the house with Nan. Nan didn't answer the door. Each time he pressed the doorbell, a new eruption of barking broke out. Finally he waited long enough for the noise to die down, then called out, "Miss O'Flannary, our customer service would really like to know how we could've kept your patronage." It seemed like a long time with no barking while Nan waited, standing frozen and listening, watching as Mariah snuffled at the crack where the door met the jamb then stood tensed in anticipation, neck cocked and ears alert, for whatever excitement might ensue when the door opened. Nan tried to barely part the blinds and peek to see if Luke was finally gone, but he wasn't, he hadn't even turned away yet, and the blind snapped like an electric shock when Nan flinched back and released it. Luke leaned on the bell so it rang over and over like a car alarm and the dogs burst forth into a new frenzy. Next door, someone banged something metal, a spoon against a frypan or a metal pipe against a flagpole. By the time all the noise died down, Luke's truck had already screeched backwards up the driveway.

Maybe it was the new water company delivery truck that dented her mailbox. Her driveway was always difficult to maneuver, and the new driver was inexperienced. She changed services again, this time to a built-in water purification system which only needed to be serviced once a year.

Twice a day Nan walked up her driveway, in the morning for the newspaper and in the afternoon for the mail. The newspaper, always rolled inside a plastic bag, was supposed to be thrown to the black side of the double driveway, but often it had skidded to the neighbor's grey concrete. But she started finding the newspaper, almost every morning, just off the street in the gutter. She called the delivery service complaint number a couple of times, but the gutter delivery continued and too often she found the plastic bag filled with water, the newspaper soaked and ruined. She finally canceled the paper.

In the afternoons, the neighbors were often out tending their garden. The strip of dirt running uphill beside their driveway was still thick with squash and tomatoes, green peppers and eggplant, now also had mature dwarf fruit trees. In the summer apricots and nectarines ripened, fell and rolled down the driveway, most of the time veering right—because at the bottom where the driveways split, Nan's was steeper—so the rich-smelling fruit collected and drew flies and bees in front of Nan's garage and outbuilding. Nan picked up the bruised, sometimes split apricots and tossed them up beyond the fruit trees to the empty lot on the other side of her neighbor's driveway where ground squirrels and birds could eat them. One morning the fruit must've had an interesting trip down the driveway—instead of collecting against her curbing or in front of her garage door, four or five apricots were smashed against the front windshield of her van.

Going up for her mail, Nan started to hear the neighbor woman muttering. At first Nan thought she was grumbling to her husband in another language—the dialogue was curt and one-sided, just the woman spitting one or two words at a time. Then Nan thought she made out some of the words: "nosy" and "dirty" and "ugly." Nan contemplated answering, but a returned insult was too easy to volley. Instead Nan considered looking the woman in the eye and saying, "Cookie." Of course, she never did.

Because all three offspring Nan had kept from Mariah's first litter finished their championships—the male and one bitch finished simultaneously at under two-years-old, taking the points from the dog and bitch classes at the same shows—Mariah's entire second litter had been sold before it was whelped. People were calling to be put on the waiting list before Mariah was even bred. Then the contracted new owners had visited weekly, sometimes more than that, as the whelps grew into pups. Their reports about her neighbors were no longer throwaway comments, jokes or offhand questions. One woman said, "Do your neighbors know you have a kennel here? I think that guy next door said 'more big stink' as I walked by." Another reported that the long-skirted wife came up the driveway shouting for her to move her car, even though she was parked on Nan's black asphalt side as Nan had instructed. A man had a flat tire just blocks after leaving Nan's driveway. Someone else's car was scratched, a single unbroken line from the headlights to the rear fender on the side that was closest to the neighbor's side of the driveway. Only once or twice Luke's truck—he still delivered water to the neighbor—blocked her clients, and they had to honk to ask him to move.

But her clients had seemed to stop noticing the girl, and Nan realized the middle of the day was punctuated with a long span of relative quiet, other than whatever hammering or whirring of machinery the man was involved with in his garage or garden, and the cackle of chickens from a coop hidden on the far side of their house. On weekday mornings, very early when joggers would be using the golf course before it opened, Nan still regularly heard the girl on the next-door patio firing off strings of *Hi*. Then for an hour or so the girl would yell inside the house, long unbroken cries or shouts, the way a baby wails, but in a near adult voice, and completely sob-less. After that, at around eight when Nan would be loading Mariah and her champion son and one or two clients' dogs into the van to take them to a track where she would road-work them on her bicycle, the neighbor girl—now as tall as her mother and built thick and square, still always dressed in cotton shorts and top or sweat pants and sweatshirt—would be following a parent or one of her sisters up the drive-way, twisting her hands in front of her stomach and reciting, or shouting, *cookie*. As Nan slowed at the top of her driveway before pulling out into the street, she often saw them standing beside their mailbox. Then one day Nan had to wait because a school bus was stopped in the road block-ing the driveways, and the girl was being helped from behind to climb aboard, yelling *cookie* to the driver, and *cookie* as she lurched down the aisle toward a seat. In the afternoon, Nan started waiting until after five to get her mail, because some time between 3:30 and 4:30, without seeing the bus arrive, she would once again hear the cries of the girl as she came back down the driveway with her mother or a sister, bellowing *cookie*, which, it seemed, had mutated into a less recognizable word, something like *soo-tay*.

Animal control wouldn't tell her who filed the complaint, but the officer's unannounced inspection and list of possible violations—too many ani-mals on the property, unlicensed animals, unsanitary conditions and noise infractions—were easily dispensed with. First of all, Nan's kennel license had been grandfathered when the area was zoned as a residential neigh-borhood. There had been no neighbors, nothing but the golf course, when she first bought the lot and built here. Secondly, there were obviously no unsanitary conditions, the dogs that didn't belong to Nan often came from other counties and were either licensed there or had health certifi-cates; Nan's dog's were all properly registered; and the kennel license al-lowed her more dogs than the current laws specified.

But right around the time animal control came, indicating a "series of complaints," Nan noticed her eugenia hedge, now eight or nine feet tall and too dense to see through, was burned and dying on the side facing the neighbors. A landscaping contractor postulated the bushes had been sprayed with herbicide on that side, so Nan hired his company to replace the hedge with an eight-foot cedar fence.

As he measured the side of the lot where the fence would go, and made an estimate that included calling a surveyor to re-establish where the property boundary between Nan's lot and the neighbors actually ran, the girl was out on the patio deck chanting *Hi!* The word sounded like *aye* with just a wisp of *h* at the beginning. "I see why you need the fence," the contractor said. "I can enclose your whole lot."

Nan just said "no, thanks," and didn't try to explain that she didn't fear trespassing any more than she feared her dogs getting loose and leaving her property, and the girl next door was either penned on the patio, inside the house, or supervised in the driveway. So the fence was just erected where the hedge had been, starting from the end of Nan's driveway and extending back along the side of her house to where the embankment suddenly sloped down to the golf course fairway.

The sweet cedar scent still wafted through the windows Nan kept open throughout the house—the fence was less than a month old—when Nan heard hammering and sawing coming from that part of property line. In fact something was knocking against the fence itself. The contractor had warned her new zoning laws might stipulate that a fence could only be six feet, but since she had a kennel, he'd noted, maybe her neighbors would overlook the breach. But she had a year-old bitch from Mariah's second litter in the sink in the grooming room, almost thoroughly soaped, so Nan couldn't run to see if her fence was being razed. She not only had to work the soap through the undercoat and down to the dog's skin, she had to add the bluing shampoo to the dog's white collar and chest, then let the soap sit for five minutes for conditioning, before thoroughly rinsing, then toweling the dog with three dry towels and doing an initial blow-dry, finally put the wet dog in a pen flanked by heat lamps before she would be able to run to the fence line and see what was happening. An adjoining pen of ten-week-old puppies, Mariah's grandchildren, yapped and clamored when Nan, in one motion, turned off the dryer, put the wet dog in the heated pen, and sprinted for the doorway.

The fence was still standing. The hammering and sawing had stopped. But she could hear someone just on the other side of the fence, breathing hard and moving something, a soft scrape of wood-against-wood, something brushed a few times against the fence, then an almost imperceptible thud. But since there obviously wasn't any disaster occurring, Nan hurried back to the wet dog who needed to have her undercoat line-brushed.

Later, before dusk, after giving Mariah her game of ball, while Mariah lay like a lioness on the Serengeti surveying the territory she controlled, Nan went to the fence, and peeked around the end. A low bench had been constructed and pushed up against Nan's fence, and atop the bench sat three white beehives. No bees were visible, but it was almost dark. By the next day, Nan could see the bees' comings and goings over the top of the fence, like an almost imperceptible trail of smoke, and she noticed a few more bees always in evidence in her flowerbeds around the lawn. When she and Mariah sat quietly on the grass, she could hear a thin, low buzzing.

One day as Mariah stood poised on the edge of the embankment, using three keen senses to study something down on the golf course, slowly lifting her tail like a banner over her back, Nan got up from where she'd been reclining on her elbows and crept on her knees to the edge of the grass to see what Mariah saw. There was an unusually large group of golfers, well over the usual four. This group had four carts, probably four men actually playing golf and at least two others in sport jackets standing around without golf clubs, another had a large video camera—much bigger than the personal kind almost every dog handler used to tape and review how their dogs look in the ring—plus there were two women seated in golf carts who hadn't gotten out to swing at a ball. The man with the camera was keeping his lens trained on one of the golfers, a tall Black man wearing a chauffeur's cap backwards on his shaved head, a white shirt, baggy shorts to his knees, and two-tone golf shoes without socks. Even though she followed no sport, Nan recognized the man as a famous athlete, known all over the world—of course he would play here eventually, this was a preeminent resort golf course, bought by a Japanese conglomerate and no longer tarnished with rumors of mob-ties. This was not one of the usual times the girl next door would be outside calling "*Hi,*" but Nan suddenly wished she were, so the athlete would be prompted to look up, and he would then see Mariah—even with all his triumphs that had struck awe in the eyes of the whole world, *he'd* be struck by the dog's elegant, sublime beauty. Mariah had five all-breed Best-in-Show trophies, numerous group placements, at least thirty Best-of-Breed awards from all-breed shows and over two dozen Best-of-Breeds at specialty shows, including twice at the national specialty. Nan was considering retiring her from showing. Now seven years old, she was close to achieving seven champion offspring and could have one more litter.

It was a rare Sunday when Nan didn't have a dog-event, but Mariah had been bred for the last time and was due to whelp in two weeks. Besides, Nan hadn't liked Sunday's judging panel and had already exhibited Friday and Saturday, so she had an extra day to catch up with bills and paperwork, with weeding flowerbeds and mowing the lawn, washing dog bedding, bleaching the concrete floor of the outbuilding, and spraying around the perimeter of the property for ticks. In the late afternoon, Nan was in the kitchen making liver biscuit. She'd long since stopped using the pure boiled-then-baked liver at dog shows and now bought freeze-dried liver, ground it and added it to a biscuit recipe. She pressed the dough in a pan and baked it like brownies, but long enough to make it dry and hard so when cut into cubes it didn't crumble, and it didn't stink nearly as much as pure cooked liver. It smelled enough, though, that she always baked a pan of real brownies right after the liver biscuits, to chase the odor of liver from the house.

While the brownies cooled on the shelf and the liver biscuits cooled in the washroom, Nan roused Mariah from a nap on the sofa, and they slipped through the slider to the fresher air of the lawn that over-looked the golf course. It should have been ethereal and tranquil. Sunday afternoons, when Nan returned from a show, were usually—and thankfully—refreshing times for a nap because the neighbors spent all day somewhere else, possibly at church, until past nine at night, so there was no pounding or chopping, no sweeping or digging or sawing or motorized leaf mulcher; no sound like the scraping of shingles from the roof and hammering on of new ones that had gone on most of last week. And no yelling. When the family came home from whatever they did all of Sunday, Nan was usually getting ready for bed—the car would pull in, doors open, and immediately it began: *soo-tay, soo-tay, sooooo-tay*! and "Come on, Maria, be quiet," footsteps in hard-heeled shoes on the concrete, until they were inside, maybe just the man remaining out in the garage, some small sound of tinkering, as though inventing something to do to keep himself from having to go inside too.

But that Sunday afternoon was not quiet. Nan didn't know why she hadn't noticed while inside baking, but the girl was outside on the neighbor's patio, and her shouts were markedly different that usual. Usually she only said "Hi," while on the patio, but it was the other word Nan was hearing. It had mutated again, toot-say, toot-say, toot-say. The girl repeated it faster than her normal rhythm, with an edge of panic in her voice, then ceased the word for a series of continuous wordless cries, like howling except there was no *oooo*, it was more *aaahhhhhhh, aaahhhhhh*. Then back to *toot-say, toot-say, toot-say*, and there was a low thudding sound. Even Mariah noticed the difference in what had essentially been white noise for around eight years. She barked, growled, then approached the fence cautiously, neck stretched low, stalking catlike, so unlike her

customary bold demeanor. Nan followed slowly, staying behind Mariah
to watch her.

Aaahhhhhhh, aaahhhhhhh, toot-say, toot-saaaaaay! The voice more feral
and raw, but still without the wet sound of tears, the thumping faster but
no louder. Mariah advanced along the fence-line toward the end then
stood with tail up and bristled but head very low, trying to use her nose
instead of her eyes to explain the disturbance she heard. Holding onto
the end of the fence, Nan also crouched low and leaned around, her body
hovering above Mariah's.

The girl was in pajamas. The thumping was the glass slider rattling
because she was violently pulling on the handle, as though trying to open
it like a regular door. Then she left the glass, turned and walked to the
railing, hands waving about her face, calling rapid-fire, *toot-say, toot-say,
toot-say, toot-say!* The current of bees leaving and returning to the three
hives seemed a little more visible, and perhaps less orderly as though some
bees were circling, unsure whether to come back or venture out. But, un-
der the girl's commotion, Nan didn't know if the bees were buzzing any
louder. From what she could see, the girl seemed huge, her head enor-
mous, her hair tangled and awry, her eyes thin slits in a very round high-
cheeked face, but whether this was from bee stings or her genetic appear-
ance, Nan couldn't tell. It had been too long since she'd taken a long,
direct look at the girl. She must be fifteen or sixteen years old by now.

A bee buzzed close, zooming past Nan's ears. She backed up, took
Mariah by the collar and pulled her back too. "Come on, girl, let's not get
your babies in an uproar." She brought Mariah inside the house. *Toot-say,
toot-say, toot-say.* The cries were more muffled. The thudding, if the girl
returned to rattle the glass slider, couldn't be heard at all. Mariah stood
outside the washroom, bright eyes back and forth between the door and
Nan's face, shifting her bulky weight from left to right on her back feet—
ultrasound had predicted she was carrying five or six whelps—then she
whined a perky sound and stamped one of her front feet. Finally she
barked: not an alarm, a requisition. Nan laughed and went to cut a liver
biscuit for her from the pan in the washroom.

Toot-say, toot-say, aaahhhhhhh, aaahhhhhhh!

Nan looked up and paused, cleaning the knife blade between her thumb
and index finger. Mariah was vacuuming the last crumbs from her biscuit
from the floor at her feet.

Soo-tay, soo-tay, hi, hi, hi, soo-tay, aaahhhhhhh!

Nan made two or three swift cuts across the brownies both ways, left the knife in the sink and took the whole pan of brownies. Mariah tried to follow, but Nan told her to stay and shut the slider as Mariah's nose tried to slip into the shrinking opening. Then Mariah hit the glass with her front feet and barked in mock anger.

As soon as she spotted Nan coming around the fence, the girl's voice modulated. "Hi." She paused. "Hi." Once on the neighbor's side, Nan had to make her away past the bee hives, then through some straggly geraniums growing amid loose rocks, then bare ground and plenty of foxtails. Around the base of the neighbor's raised redwood patio was a curved row of cauliflower and purple cabbage and tall rubbery stalks that appeared to be the tops of onions. Nan stepped between the plants, her head level with the floor of the deck.

The girl said, "Hi."

"Hi," Nan answered, standing below her, then lifted the pan of brownies and the girl reached down to take it.

At first Nan didn't see the policeman come around the corner of the neighbor's property. The girl's mouth was too full to speak, crumbs caking her lips and cheeks, a big ragged piece of brownie in each hand. Nan waited below for the empty pan.

Nan startled when the officer said, "Hello? Everything all right here?"

The girl didn't respond. The policeman was beside the corner of the house, more on the same level as the deck. Nan raised her hand. "Down here."

"You live here?"

"No. Next door."

"We received a call from the resort about a problem here, someone screaming." Then he looked up at the girl. "Retarded?"

"Yes."

"Where're her folks? They leave her alone here?"

Nan hesitated before answering. Then the girl said "Hi." Crumbs flew from her mouth. Nan reached up and pushed the pan back and forth on the floor of the deck to draw the girl's attention back to the brownies. "Just this once," Nan said softly. "Maybe there was some emergency. They must've forgotten she was out here."

"Looks like she's wet herself. She's still in pajamas."

"Very unusual," Nan murmured.

"She pregnant?"

Nan looked up sharply. Looming above her, the girl was large and thickset. Her big thighs and arms were fleshy, and she had ample, mature breasts. Her midsection was as bulky as any of the rest of her. Nan could smell chocolate and the urine on the girl's pajamas. "I don't think so." Nan's voice was still feathery, although her heart thudded.

"I'll have to have someone check her out," the policeman said, but Nan had already turned, leaving the brownie pan, and was making her way through the geraniums and the flow of bees toward the fence.

It was almost two months later the neighbor woman rang Nan's doorbell.

But before that, for the first several weeks, Nan had felt herself awaiting the next shoe to drop, tiptoeing around the house and compound, alert to any clang or rustle from next door, shushing the dogs more often, keeping them inside in the crates more of the day, and often caught herself listening for the cry of a newborn. Whenever she heard a vehicle on the driveway, she had put down whatever she was doing and had gone to the nearest door or window to check, watchful for any sign of subsequent official action—child-protective services, additional police involvement, public heath or social workers—and for any clue that might denote increased rancor. She especially checked the lawn over-looking the golf course each time before allowing Mariah out there. Despite the fence, it was the only spot, besides the adjoined driveways, were the neighbors had easy access to her property. She looked for pieces of bread or crackers, dog biscuits, even pieces of meat or soup bones on her lawn. But Mariah wanted to go out less and less as her whelping time drew near. It still took some time after the pups arrived for Nan's vigilant preoccupation to snap.

Mariah's last litter of five pups were four weeks old and beginning to wean when Nan noticed Mariah leaving food in her bowl, even though, while nursing, the high-protein kibble was mixed with yogurt. Nan realized she'd been preparing the meals as usual, but without Mariah at her feet, urging her to hurry. She opened a special canned diet for lactating bitches and filled Mariah's bowl. The pups clamoring at her nipples, Mariah walked away, humped over, retching, but the vomit was not the sort produced by a dam for weaning pups to eat. It was bile, and not even the usual bright yellow. This was a foul brown.

Yes, it could be a slow poisoning, the vet said, but on his initial palpation of Mariah's abdomen, he felt something right away, an enlarged liver he said at first, but it was probably standard procedure to not say cancer until the x-ray and ultrasound were performed and the diagnosis confirmed: Lymphoma that had already metastasized. No recommendation of surgery, the liver was already overwhelmed, and the pancreas, stomach and gall bladder were affected.

Facing the vet, Nan stood at the stainless steel examination table where Mariah reclined with her head up, relaxed and panting gently, in a leisured posture as though stretched out serenely at a spa for her weekly massage, seemingly drowsy and content. "But . . ." Words had to be squeezed slowly through Nan's constricted throat, one at a time, ". . . she never . . ." and the vet waited, his hand slowly stroking Mariah from her neck to her ribs, "I mean . . . she didn't . . . kill her puppies."

"Yes, remarkable. But she has no knowledge of what cancer is. She doesn't know she's terminal."

"But . . . all this time . . . it must've been . . ." Nan's eyes stayed on the vet's hand moving over what was left of Mariah's burnt-red coat after being shaved for the ultrasound, ". . . and she never showed . . . anything. Unless. I didn't . . . notice . . ."

"Some dogs have huge pain thresholds," he said. "Their drive to continue being the dog they always were is much stronger than any debilitation-driven impulse to let down and admit they can't. Until they really can't."

And a week later—her body shaved in more ragged patches to allow IV attachment, still eating nothing, vomiting viscous sputum and peeing blood—this time completely devoid of any remaining poise or vigor, lying with head down in her own foam bed on the examination table, while Nan cupped Mariah's face and pressed her nose to Mariah's perfect muzzle, the vet injected an overdose of an anesthetic agent, and Mariah quietly surrendered her final breath.

When the doorbell rang, every dog, de-barked or not, went ballistic. In both hands the neighbor woman held Nan's brownie pan, washed clean. In the middle of the pan were two peanut butter jars with wax paper between the lip of the jar and the screw top. The jars were filled with a dark amber, almost brown substance resembling transparent sap that has dried while dripping down a tree trunk.

"For thanks," the woman said, smiling. There were gaps between every one of her small teeth. Her babushka was brown and white and matched a homemade-looking shawl across her shoulders. "Fence good. Protect bee from wind. Finally make honey."

Nan had one hand on her forehead, holding dirty hair from her eyes, then waved vaguely in the direction of the still-barking dogs in the runs. "Sorry about the noise."

"We like," the woman said, "Good protect." She held the pan further out and Nan felt herself reach to accept it. Then the weight was balanced in her own hands.

"Have in tea. Feel better," the neighbor said, turning to go. "Have with more chocolate cookie you make."

Nan took the honey to the kitchen where most of the linoleum floor was taken up with a pen holding Mariah's six-week-old puppies. She lit the burner under the kettle and stood staring at the glowing electric coils until the kettle whistled, causing a chorus of aggressive yaps from the brash whelps. After dunking a teabag, Nan unscrewed one of the jars and dipped a spoon into the dark gluey honey, let it drizzle into her tea, then caught the stream of honey with two fingers, reached down and let the eager pups lick and bite the sticky sweetness from her skin. Their jubilant tails wagged straight up over their backs.

Cris Mazza is the author of over a dozen books. Her fiction titles include *Waterbaby* and *Homeland*, plus the critically celebrated story collection *Is It Sexual Harassment Yet?*, and the PEN Nelson Algren Award winning novel *How to Leave a Country*. She also has a collection of personal essays, *Indigenous: Growing Up Californian*. A native of Southern California, Mazza grew up in San Diego. Currently she lives 50 miles west of Chicago and is a professor in the Program for Writers at the University of Illinois at Chicago.